CW01637685

GIRL EIGHT: HUN TED

(A Maya Gray Mystery—Book 8)

Molly Black

Molly Black

Bestselling author Molly Black is author of the MAYA GRAY FBI suspense thriller series, comprising nine books (and counting); of the RYLIE WOLF FBI suspense thriller series, comprising six books; of the TAYLOR SAGE FBI suspense thriller series, comprising eight books; of the KATIE WINTER FBI suspense thriller series, comprising eleven books (and counting); of the RUBY HUNTER FBI suspense thriller series, comprising five books (and counting); of the CAITLIN DARE FBI suspense thriller series, comprising five books (and counting); of the REESE LINK mystery series, comprising five books (and counting); and of the CLAIRE KING mystery series, comprising five books (and counting).

An avid reader and lifelong fan of the mystery and thriller genres, Molly loves to hear from you, so please feel free to visit www.mollyblackauthor.com to learn more and stay in touch.

ISBN: 978-1-0943-3104-1

BOOKS BY MOLLY BLACK

MAYA GRAY MYSTERY SERIES
GIRL ONE: MURDER (Book #1)
GIRL TWO: TAKEN (Book #2)
GIRL THREE: TRAPPED (Book #3)
GIRL FOUR: LURED (Book #4)
GIRL FIVE: BOUND (Book #5)
GIRL SIX: FORSAKEN (Book #6)
GIRL SEVEN: CRAVED (Book #7)
GIRL EIGHT: HUNTED (Book #8)
GIRL NINE: GONE (Book #9)

RYLIE WOLF FBI SUSPENSE THRILLER
FOUND YOU (Book #1)
CAUGHT YOU (Book #2)
SEE YOU (Book #3)
WANT YOU (Book #4)
TAKE YOU (Book #5)
DARE YOU (Book #6)

TAYLOR SAGE FBI SUSPENSE THRILLER
DON'T LOOK (Book #1)
DON'T BREATHE (Book #2)
DON'T RUN (Book #3)
DON'T FLINCH (Book #4)
DON'T REMEMBER (Book #5)
DON'T TELL (Book #6)

KATIE WINTER FBI SUSPENSE THRILLER
SAVE ME (Book #1)
REACH ME (Book #2)
HIDE ME (Book #3)
BELIEVE ME (Book #4)

HELP ME (Book #5)
FORGET ME (Book #6)
HOLD ME (Book #7)
PROTECT ME (Book #8)
REMEMBER ME (Book #9)
CATCH ME (Book #10)
WATCH ME (Book #11)

RUBY HUNTER FBI SUSPENSE THRILLER
IF I RUN (Book #1)
IF I TELL (Book #2)
IF I LIVE (Book #3)
IF I FORGET (Book #4)
IF I RETURN (Book #5)

CAITLIN DARE FBI SUSPENSE THRILLER
COME GET ME (Book #1)
COME FIND ME (Book #2)
COME TAKE ME (Book #3)
COME CATCH ME (Book #4)
COME SAVE ME (Book #5)

REESE LINK MYSTERY
BEYOND REASON (Book #1)
BEYOND REACH (Book #2)
BEYOND REPAIR (Book #3)
BEYOND DOUBT (Book #4)
BEYOND NORMAL (Book #5)

CLAIRE KING MYSTERY
ONCE HE SEES (Book #1)
ONCE HE LONGS (Book #2)
ONCE HE TAKES (Book #3)
ONCE HE FEELS (Book #4)
ONCE HE KNOWS (Book #5)

CHAPTER ONE

Howie was nervous as he reached the shore of the lake. This wasn't the kind of thing he usually did. Normally, when he went out on a first date, it was to a restaurant or the movies. Or he just invited the woman straight back to his place for a simple hookup. Howie liked it when things were straightforward, when he and his dates didn't pretend that they were there for anything else.

This was somewhere in between. Raquel had been clear enough online about what she wanted, and Howie had liked that; but what she wanted also included meeting up with him down by the lake rather than just coming over to his place, or better yet, him going over to hers. It was always easier in the long run when hookups didn't know where he lived. It prevented things from getting complicated in case they thought the situation was more than it was. He was only twenty-six; he wasn't looking for some long relationship.

The shore of the lake was largely deserted at this time of night, whereas it would have been busy with tourists and locals by day. The water stretched out, pristine and still, all the way to the island that sat in the middle of the lake.

A few boats were beached next to the water, while a couple of shacks stood along the shoreline, there to sell beer, fishing supplies, or local crafts. Howie didn't care about those, except perhaps because Raquel might have the idea of going into one of them, or maybe taking one of the boats.

Either way, it was a hint of danger that added some spice to all of this. That had been why Howie was prepared to go along. Excitement, new experiences, counted for a lot.

Or they would if Raquel ever showed up. There didn't seem to be any sign of her. That worried Howie a little. Had she gotten cold feet? Or maybe this was her idea of a joke, getting him to come out to somewhere this deserted without showing up.

Then he spotted the note, pinned to a post underneath a light outside one of the shacks. It had his name written on it, in a delicate, feminine hand. Howie grabbed the note, taking it as a good sign. No one would go to the trouble of coming here and leaving a note if they weren't going to show up. They would just wait and send a message, or ghost him completely.

Not that women did that to him. Howie was good looking, a little taller than average, dark-haired, with features that seemed both youthful and rugged at once. He worked out, he knew how to dress, and more importantly, he knew how to construct an online profile to attract maximum attention.

He reached out and took the note, tearing it open confidently.

I hope you're looking forward to this as much as I am. I've prepared a spot for us on the island, where no one can see us, but we can see them. There's a rowboat on the shore you can use to get to me. I'll be waiting for you. I'm already thinking of the things I want to do to you.

R.

That was enough to spur Howie to head over to the boats near the shore, looking for the one that Raquel meant. Not that it made much difference to him by now. He would have "borrowed" another one if that was what it took to get to Raquel at this point. The pictures she'd sent him online had been… well, they made all this worth it.

It didn't take Howie long to find a single rowboat tied up in the water, with oars left in it waiting for him. He got in and took them up, rowing out toward the island with powerful strokes.

The island was one of those places that everyone went; it was lightly wooded, with a series of strange statues there that were partly art, partly there to scare the kids. There were things built to look ancient but were actually modern constructions, up to and including a tower that had been built to look half-ruined from the start. There were sheltered spots that kids or anglers had put in place for when the weather was bad, but tonight it was clear and warm. The moon was out, providing plenty of light.

Howie was making good time, cutting through the water smoothly as he got closer to the island, closer to Raquel. He could imagine her watching him approaching, probably enjoying the sight of him making so much physical effort to get to her.

Howie reached the shore of the island and pulled the boat up onto a pebbly beach, using his phone as a flashlight so that he could see what he was doing.

He didn't need to. There was a row of candles set out, each leading to the next in an obvious trail. They looked like they'd been burning for a little while, but they spurred him on. He followed them along what looked like a well-worn path, toward the half-ruined tower.

The tower sat on the far shore. The trail led to it and then around it, to a spot where a blanket had been laid down, a bottle of wine and a picnic hamper sitting on it.

There was no sign of Raquel, though, and Howie frowned at that. She should be there. This was clearly the spot where she wanted to meet him, so shouldn't she have been waiting?

Or maybe she was planning to surprise him? Maybe this was all part of the fun. Still, Howie found himself looking around for her.

"Raquel? Raquel, are you there?"

He looked around, trying to find any sign of her, growing more worried by the moment. Had she gotten cold feet? Had something happened to her? No, he had to believe that this was all some big part of whatever scenario Raquel had planned for the evening. He checked the tower, but there was no sign of her there. He checked back at the blanket, but she hadn't shown up while he was away.

There *were* a couple more candles, leading to the shoreline. One floated there as part of a paper lantern, providing additional light. Howie went over to it, staring, trying to make sense of it. He could see his reflection in the water, and there, beyond it, something else.

At first, it seemed to be like some strange, extra reflection, some shadow-self there on the surface. Then, he saw a figure, another man.

He barely had an instant to respond before that figure moved, and a thin cord wrapped around his throat, pulling tight.

CHAPTER TWO

Maya went up to Marco's apartment, knowing that she owed him an apology.

She was still wearing her dark work suit, her tall frame and long legs taking the stairs of Marco's apartment building two at a time. She brushed a strand of dark hair back out of her eyes as she went.

She'd been hard on him. When he'd suggested that she was pushing too hard and taking too many risks, she'd told him that if he didn't like the way she was obsessing over trying to find her sister, then he could go back to Cleveland and leave her team.

Maya didn't mean that. She didn't want to do this without him. She wanted him there with her, both professionally and, yes, personally.

That didn't mean that Maya was going to give up on trying to find her sister. Megan's safety came before everything and she was still in the hands of a serial killer along with other women the Moonlight Killer had kidnapped to force Maya to work on cases for him. But she did want to make this right with Marco.

Maya kept moving up through his apartment building, trying to rehearse what she was going to say to him. She would start with an apology, try to set out why she felt that she had to keep going with all of this, but also try to make it clear to him how much she cared and that she wanted him to be a part of her life.

Maya was still running through all the ways the conversation could go in her mind when she reached Marco's apartment and saw that the door was hanging open. Instantly, Maya was worried. She knew that Marco wouldn't leave the door to his apartment open like that, so something had to be wrong. Was his apartment being robbed?

Or was it something worse?

Maya drew her weapon, the Glock feeling natural against the palm of her hand even as her heart rate went up. She wanted to just charge in there, but her military and FBI training made her move more carefully, approaching the door and using the frame for cover as she kicked it open and looked inside, trying to check all the angles.

She couldn't see any burglars or other bad guys in there, but she *could* see a figure lying there on the floor, blood pooling around him.

"Marco!" Maya called out. She ran to him without thinking about it, then found herself instinctively checking the room, knowing that it could still be a trap.

The moment she heard Marco groan in pain, all of Maya's attention went back to him.

He normally looked so strong and so boyishly handsome with his tall swimmer's frame and his sandy blonde hair. Now, pain contorted his features and bruises covered his face. They were nothing, though, compared to the patch of darkening blood staining his shirt.

Maya knew a gunshot wound when she saw one, and immediately moved to put pressure on it, trying to keep as much precious lifeblood inside Marco as she could. A part of her wanted to check how bad the wound was, and if the bullet had gone through, but the field medicine skills she'd picked up in military intelligence also told her that the worst thing she could do right then was try to move him.

Maya called 911, hearing the terror in her own voice as she spoke to the operator.

"My name is Agent Maya Gray, with the FBI. I need an ambulance to my location ASAP, along with local police. My partner has been shot."

She put the phone down. Maya saw something lying beside Marco then. A postcard. One with a single wounded bunny rabbit drawn on it. Keeping pressure on Marco's wound, Maya flipped it over.

Just you from now on, Dear Maya. No more help.

Fury replaced the fear in Maya then for a moment or two. The Moonlight Killer was behind this. He'd done this, or he'd had someone do this.

She would make sure that he paid for it.

*

Maya ran into the hospital, unable to keep the fear out of her heart as she did so. They hadn't let her ride in the ambulance, and worse, she'd had to stay at Marco's apartment, securing the scene until more agents arrived.

Those had been the most frustrating minutes of her life. More than minutes, it had been hours now since she'd found him. Hours of answering questions and following procedures when all she'd wanted was to be here. She'd wanted to be by his side, but she couldn't be.

She headed up to the reception desk, where a harassed looking woman in her forties seemed to be dealing with a line of people.

Under any other circumstances, Maya would have waited in that line patiently, would have let everyone else take their turn, but these weren't normal circumstances. This was about Marco.

"Marco Spinelli, where is he?" she demanded.

"I'm sorry, ma'am, you'll have to wait in line."

Maya slammed her badge down on the reception desk. Marco was in danger. There was no time to hesitate in a situation like this.

"Which room is Detective Marco Spinelli in?" Maya asked. "He's my partner."

The receptionist looked as though she might argue, even then. One look at Maya's expression made her think better of it.

"Room 304."

Maya ran for the elevators. She knew that nothing she could do now would make a difference in how this turned out, but she still felt as though she had to get there, had to be by his side.

On the floor where Marco's room was situated, Maya spotted a couple of agents hanging around, obviously making sure that no one got to Marco. She recognized Agent Reyes, her sometime nemesis from the department and Agent Harris's right-hand man. Reyes was a Latino man in his twenties, with dark hair and a serious expression, currently wearing slacks and a shirt with the holster for his weapon clearly visible as if to scare off any potential threats.

"Gray," he said as Maya approached. "Harris wants to know what's going on."

"What's going on is that my partner was attacked in his own apartment," Maya snapped back at him. She didn't like Reyes, even if she was grateful that he was there helping to keep Marco safe. He was always too interested in his own advancement for Maya to really trust him.

"He'll want a report." Trust Reyes to put how Harris would react ahead of the fact that Marco was in the hospital.

"Not *now*, Reyes," Maya said, and pushed past her fellow agent to get to the hospital room. She didn't have to answer to Harris anyway; she was the head of her own small task force now, hunting the "kidnapper" who had taken her sister and who was making her solve cases to see his captives released.

The problem would come if Harris insisted on looking too closely at all of this. If he ever found out that the kidnapper was the notorious serial killer known as the Moonlight Killer, Maya would lose control of the investigation at the very least, if she didn't lose her job in the bargain for holding the information back.

For now, though, none of that mattered to Maya. All that mattered was getting to Marco. She reached the door of room 304, looked in, and felt a wave of relief hit her as she saw Marco sitting up in bed in a hospital gown.

Maya hurried over to him and threw her arms around him, only pulling back when she heard a sound of pain from him.

"Sorry," Maya said. "I should have thought."

"From what I hear, you're the main reason I'm still alive," Marco said. He smiled at her. "How do I look?"

Maya tilted her head sideways. "Honestly? Awful. You look like you were beaten to within an inch of your life and then shot."

He had bruises all over his face. One eye was swollen almost shut. His knuckles were bandaged, but there was some blood seeping through. Then there were the bandages on his side, covering the gunshot wound that had come so close to killing him.

"Pretty accurate," Marco replied, obviously trying to make a joke of it. His voice sounded weaker than usual.

"What happened?" Maya asked.

"Someone used a recording of your voice to trick me into answering the door. They attacked me, then they shot me."

There was no emotion in his voice as he said that, like he was just giving a statement. Probably he already had. Reyes wouldn't just be there to keep watch. The news was enough to break Maya's heart. They'd used her voice to get to him. If he hadn't been around her, he wouldn't even have been a target.

"Are you all right, Marco?" Maya asked. "I was expecting to get here and find you still in surgery."

"The bullet was through and through," Marco said, with a wince. "It didn't hit any major organs, but they had to work to stop the bleeding. They've got it stopped now and stitched me up, but I don't think I'll be going anywhere for a while."

He still sounded so matter of fact about it all, but maybe that was his way of coping with all of this, as if letting Maya see how much it had scared him would only make him feel worse.

His expression did soften a little then, though. "You saved my life, Maya. If you hadn't come by…"

"I think I'm also the reason that you were hurt in the first place," Maya said. She took out the postcard. "This was left next to you. I'm sorry, Marco. He did this, or had this done, to stop you from helping me."

"He's trying to draw you deeper into this sick game of his," Marco pointed out.

Maya nodded. "I know, but I'm not sure I have a lot of choice. He still has my sister. I still need to find a way to end this."

Marco reached out, taking Maya's arm, even though it obviously hurt to do so. "You need to be careful, Maya. The guy… he had me. He could have shot me in the head as easily as in the gut. He could have killed me."

The implication being that he could do the same to Maya just as easily.

"I understand the danger, Marco," she said.

"Do you, though?" he countered. "This is a serial killer you're dealing with. He's utterly ruthless, and he's already shown how good he is at what he does."

"I know that," Maya said. "But you must know that I can't just give up. Not when he still has Megan and the other women."

"I know," Marco said. "I'm just telling you that I want you to be careful. What if he's getting me out of the way so that he can have a clear shot at you?"

That was a possibility, and a terrifying one. So far, the Moonlight Killer had played his twisted game according to its rules, but Maya had no doubt about how it would end. The two of them were hunting one another at the same time, each in their own way, and if Maya didn't find a way to take the Moonlight Killer down, there was a good chance that she would end up dead.

Maya clenched her hands into fists. "Then he'd better not miss."

CHAPTER THREE

The man they called Frank sat at the heart of his bunker, watching his remaining bunnies on the monitors he'd set up in the grand circular space of his control room and wondering which of them he should pick to be the prize for his next game with dear Maya.

There weren't many of them left now, only five, moving around the place in their identical gray jumpsuits, twitching at every sound as if they feared that it might be him coming to kill one of them.

No, he had to push that thought from his mind, because it made the possibility all too tempting. These women might fit the pattern he'd established for himself, all young and fragile, all delicately pretty, all on the cusp of change in their lives, but they were not here for him to simply kill as part of his other… work. They were his leverage, his way of getting Maya Gray to continue working to clear his name of crimes that had nothing to do with him.

Little by little, she was solving the cases he wanted, clearing away the detritus to leave the pristine, beautiful pattern of his true work there for all to see. It wasn't quite visible to the world yet, though, which meant that the two of them would need to do more together.

He wondered how angry Maya would be with him that he'd had the man she was romantically involved with hurt. He knew that his experience of emotions wasn't the same as other people, that they weren't in control of them the way Frank was. He understood enough about the emotions of ordinary people to manipulate them, and he guessed that in this case, Maya would be filled with anger.

It wouldn't stop her from doing what he wanted, though. Not while he had her sister as his captive.

Frank watched her on the monitors. She looked so like her sister with the same dark hair and fine bone structure, yet where Maya seemed strong, she was willowy and delicate. She was tougher than she looked, though. Frank knew that it was her who went to the others and kept their spirits up, her who tried to keep them from giving in to despair.

Frank allowed that, because it reduced the risk that he would lose any more of his bunnies to suicide or escape attempts. He'd had enough trouble finding one replacement bunny for his collection; he had no wish to try to find another at this late stage in the game.

That game had taken so much effort already, so much preparation. Frank had used all the skills he'd learned during his time in the military to set it up and keep it running smoothly. It had cost him time, effort, and money. There had been moments when he'd thought it wasn't worth it because it meant sitting here and holding back from the things he longed to do, but in this moment, as it was all starting to come together, Frank couldn't help feeling a certain… satisfaction with it all.

Frank switched over his monitors to watch security footage from the hospital room where they had put Detective Marco Spinelli. The feed from them had been easy enough to hack into, letting him watch as Maya stood near his bed, reaching out an arm to touch his shoulder tenderly.

That sent a flicker of anger through Frank. No, not anger, something stranger, something that he barely understood. Jealousy.

He was jealous of this policeman who had become more than dear Maya's partner. Jealous enough that for a moment he found himself wishing that his associate had killed the detective rather than merely wounding him. Of course, that would have gone against Frank's instructions. Frank had considered Maya and decided that killing Spinelli outright ran too high a risk of her refusing to do more work for him, or throwing herself wholeheartedly into trying to hunt him down.

Frank pushed the feelings aside. This way was better. The detective had been eliminated from the equation neatly enough, Maya had been reminded of the power that Frank had to reach out and touch her life, and the balance of their game had been restored, without the help that the detective had been giving her.

That game made for a relationship between the two of them that was utterly intimate in its own way. Frank knew Maya better than anyone else at this point. He watched her life through his associates; he listened to her phone calls. He had her running around at his beck and call, doing everything he said. Using her sister, he could make her feel fear or hope, joy, or despair.

Perhaps at the end of all this, the game would finish in the most intimate way of all, with his rope around Maya Gray's neck.

Not now, though. Not while she still had work to do for him. Frank had already picked out his next case for her to solve, the next smear on his name that had to be removed.

He took out a postcard and started to draw, copying the image of the hospital room, the positioning of Maya and her beloved. He drew them as bunnies, of course, to fit the theme that he had chosen, and to emphasize to her that Maya was potential prey just as much as the others.

The whole world divided into predators and prey, and he sat at the apex of all of it. Frank drew carefully, then turned over to set out the details of the case he wanted Maya to look at. As usual, he found himself conflicted, half hoping that she would solve it, half hoping that she would fail and give him a reason to kill one of the waiting bunnies.

He finished it with a flourish. It was time for his great work to continue.

CHAPTER FOUR

As much as Maya hated leaving Marco, she couldn't stay there by his bedside all day. She had to leave to keep working on trying to catch the man responsible for putting him there, and for kidnapping her sister.

She didn't head back to the FBI's offices immediately, though. Instead, there was one other person in the hospital Maya needed to see first. She walked over to the room where Saoirse O'Dell was recuperating from her time as the Moonlight Killer's captive. She'd been the last one to be released by him, after Maya and Marco had solved the previous case he'd sent them on.

There weren't any police outside her room anymore. Perhaps that was because they'd been diverted to protect Marco, or perhaps they thought that Saoirse was no longer in danger. Either way, Maya resolved to bring it up with Harris when she saw him.

For now, the important part was trying to find something, anything, that would let her get closer to catching the man responsible for all of this.

When Maya entered the room, Saoirse was sitting up in bed, looking restless, like she would rather have been anywhere else but there in the hospital. Maya guessed that it wouldn't be long before she discharged herself and tried to get back to whatever kind of normal life she could find.

The young woman looked pale and drained by her experience of captivity. Her red hair was a mess, and there was something frightened about the way her green eyes darted around the room, looking for danger.

When those eyes fixed on Maya, there was a flicker of fear mixed in with gratitude.

"Agent Gray, what are you doing here?"

"I wanted to see how you were," Maya said. She didn't want to press too quickly for the information she needed. This was a young woman who had been through a lot.

"They say that I'm physically ok," Saoirse said. "But they want me to talk to a counselor. Every time I close my eyes, it's like I'm back there."

Maya could only imagine what it had been like for her, trapped in a bunker with the other women, prey to the whims of a serial killer. Maya had seen pictures of how violently he could react to any infraction against his game. He'd systematically beaten her sister, Megan, as retribution for an attempted raid to catch him.

Saoirse looked over at Maya with a hint of anger. "You're Megan's sister. You're the reason that all of this is happening."

That made a wave of guilt rise in Maya because it was true, at least up to a point. The Moonlight Killer had taken Megan, had taken Saoirse, had taken all of them, because he wanted leverage to make her do everything that he wanted. He knew about Maya's skills with cold cases and had looked for a way to force her to use them to clear his name in cases that had nothing to do with him.

It was almost as if it mattered to him that the world saw the truth of what he had done, without anything to distract from it.

"The man who took you is the reason this is happening," Maya said. "All I'm trying to do is get you and the others back safely."

Saoirse was silent for several seconds after that. She nodded. "I thought… back in there, I thought that he wasn't really letting us go. I thought that he just killed one of us each time and pretended that he'd released us. I thought Megan was so naive for believing that he would do what he said."

Maya saw the young woman shudder as she said that. She could only imagine what it had been like for her, being sure that she would die there in the place where the Moonlight Killer had kept them all.

"Did Megan… tell you anything?" Maya asked. "Did she give you anything to pass on to me?"

Previously, Megan had sent women out with fragments of information that she'd managed to glean by observing the environment around her in the place where she and the others were imprisoned. One young woman had been sent with the information that Megan had heard a saw-whet owl, which had helped to narrow down the locations they might have been held. Maya was hoping for more hints like that.

To her disappointment, though, Saoirse shook her head.

"She kept looking around the bunker, all the time. It was like she wanted to make sure she hadn't missed some tiny detail, something she could use. But *he* made sure that there was nothing. He was always in control of it all."

"This is the man who held you captive?" Maya said. She had to be careful not to refer to him as the Moonlight Killer. That was a piece of information that only she and Marco knew, and if it got out, then she was certain that she would no longer be the one running the hunt for him.

"That's right," Saoirse said. "He was always so careful, always wore a mask and gloves, always kept hidden any sign of where we were being kept. He made it so there was no way for us to even begin to pick up clues about what was going on there."

Or if he had, then they were either planted things or things that led nowhere. He'd let one of his captives smell a particular perfume as she was released, leading to a raid on an abandoned perfume factory. Another had seen a tattoo linked to a particular special forces unit, but there were so many men out there with that tattoo that it did nothing to narrow down the search for the killer. There were moments when Maya felt as though she was chasing a ghost, never able to catch up to him, never able to find out anything solid about him.

"What was it you were planning to do before he grabbed you?" Maya asked. That was another intriguing aspect of the case: the Moonlight Killer liked to target young women on the cusp of some great change in their lives.

Saoirse looked at Maya in surprise. "How… how did you know? I was planning to move across the country, change my whole life, do an MFA. Now… now I don't know what I'm going to do."

Maya could see the tears in her eyes then and the fear that went along with them. In that sense, it seemed that the Moonlight Killer had robbed her of that great change in her future as clearly as if he'd strangled her like all his other victims.

Maya put a hand on Saoirse's arm. "You can still do all of that. This isn't going to be the thing that defines your life, Saoirse. You're out of there now. It will take time, but you'll be able to take strength from this. You survived, and you can't let him stop you from doing all the things that you wanted to do."

She nodded, but Maya couldn't tell if the young woman truly believed her. She did know that she wasn't going to get anything there. Saoirse didn't know anything about the man who had kidnapped her and the others, and by continuing to press for information, Maya would just be intruding upon her pain.

"I should go," she said. "I need to get back to work."

Saoirse's hand shot out then, grabbing Maya's arm. "Promise me that you'll find a way to end this. Promise me. He's getting more unstable. It's all getting more dangerous. If you don't catch him soon, the others, your sister, might all die."

And Maya couldn't allow that. She had already sworn to herself that she would do whatever it took to keep Megan safe.

"I'm going to do everything I can," she said automatically. She glanced down at the arm holding her, trying to work out the gentlest way to disengage from Saoirse's grip.

As she did so, Maya noticed something: a rash that had spread across Saoirse's arm. It looked like a reaction to something. That was enough to puzzle Maya slightly.

"Saoirse, what happened to your arm?" she asked.

Saoirse looked at the rash for a second or two. "That? I had it when I came here. I guess I must have brushed up against something. Nettles, or poison oak, or something."

"Yes," Maya said. "But when would you have done that, if you were being kept indoors?"

She saw Saoirse trying to think, her brow furrowing with the effort of trying to remember.

"I… I think I remember brushing up against something as he took me out of there to put me in a van. Before he drugged me. I remember that my arm started itching."

Meaning that there was a good chance that this had happened right outside the spot where he was holding the women. If the rash could be identified as being from a particular plant, then maybe it could help Maya to narrow down the location.

"Can I take a look at your chart?" Maya asked.

"Sure, I guess. What are you looking for?"

"I'm hoping the doctors have identified what the rash is from," Maya said. "Maybe it will help me work out what the plants are around the place where he held you."

Maya took the chart, looking for any sign of the rash on it. Saoirse had been exhausted and malnourished when she came in, in need of fluids and rest. There was a note about the rash. It wasn't from poison oak, or ivy, or anything else that was common enough for the doctors to identify it.

That gave Maya a hint of hope, because if the plant was something rare, then that meant that it wouldn't grow in a bunch of locations. Finding it might significantly narrow down the areas where the Moonlight Killer was holding the women.

"Can I take a picture of this rash?" Maya asked. She took out her phone to do it, then thought better of it. If the Moonlight Killer had full access to her phone, he might see the photograph and know that Maya was getting closer to him. That might put her sister in more danger.

Maya stared at the rash instead, trying to memorize the nuances of it, trying to make sure that she would know it again if she saw it. She would make notes by hand as soon as she was out of here.

She just had to hope that it would help. Would this be the piece of evidence that would let Maya find the Moonlight Killer? Maya could only pray that it was, but for now, she had to get back home and start looking.

CHAPTER FIVE

Maya was angry and frustrated as she strode into the spartan, almost empty space of her apartment. She could feel her anger at everything that had happened to Marco.

The thought of it made her check every space in her apartment. It didn't take long. She went behind the small kitchen counter, checked the bathroom for anyone hiding there, went around every inch of it to make sure that there wasn't anyone waiting there to attack her the way that they'd attacked Marco.

Maya didn't think that it was likely, though. The Moonlight Killer's postcard had made it clear that she was meant to work alone from now on, and that the attack was a way of making sure that he couldn't be involved.

That suggested he wasn't going to attack her too, or have her attacked. That only made Maya angrier.

She went over to the punchbag that she kept in one corner, starting to hit it, not caring that she didn't have her bag gloves on, or that she ought to be looking for answers about the rash on Saoirse's arm. Right then, she couldn't think straight, her anger clouding her judgement.

Thud, thud.

Maya slammed her fists into the bag with jabs and crosses, not caring that the impact hurt her hands. She pictured the Moonlight Killer standing there, his face a mask-covered blank.

Thud, thud.

Maya kept slamming punches, then swung in a kick, slamming her shin into the bag hard enough to make it swing. She grabbed it, driving a couple of knees.

What would it be like when she caught up to the Moonlight Killer? The tattoo on his arm said that he was ex-military, ex-special forces. As someone who had worked in military intelligence, she knew exactly how dangerous a person like that could be. This was a man who would have been trained on a variety of weapon platforms, who would be able to fight hand to hand, move unseen, and set the deadliest of traps.

Would Maya be able to take someone like that down?

Thud, thud.

Maya slammed home a couple of hooks and more pain flashed through her hands. It wasn't like her to be nervous about who a suspect was or what he could do. Right then, it didn't matter. *Whoever* the Moonlight Killer was, she would find him and she would take him down. Permanently, if necessary. Maya would do whatever it took both to get her sister back and to make sure that this killer couldn't hurt anyone else.

Maya stopped, breathing hard with the intensity of the attacks that she'd been throwing at the bag. Her hands hurt now that she'd stopped, her knuckles raw from the impact. Maya headed over to the refrigerator, getting ice to put on them while she got out her computer and started to look for any plant that might have caused the rash on Saoirse's arm.

The doctors had already said in their notes that it didn't look like a rash from poison ivy or oak, but even so, Maya checked those first. She wanted to be certain that this was going to be something that had the potential to help her in her efforts to find the Moonlight Killer, not a dead end that wasn't going to narrow it down.

It was easy enough to find pictures online of rashes from both poison oak and poison ivy. Neither seemed to match the rash on Saoirse's arm.

That was promising because it suggested that it might be rarer. The question now was how Maya was going to match that rash up to a plant or toxin. She looked up rashes from toxic plants, starting to go through image after image, trying to find something that might help her to locate the Moonlight killer.

It was slow going, because the images weren't sorted or categorized for her to skim through easily. Instead, she was working through random pictures, hoping that she would by chance come upon someone with the same rash. But there were so many variables with it, ranging from skin type to the intensity of the exposure. Maya was quickly finding it difficult to make progress.

She kept trying, though, and was still doing it when a knock came at her door.

Maya went over to it, almost opened it on instinct, and then stopped herself. Was this what had happened to Marco? Maya drew her gun, trying to be ready for any danger. She opened the door carefully, her heartbeat speeding up as she did so, trying to brace for any sudden attack.

There was no one there. There was just a postcard on the floor, waiting for her.

"Wasn't the one at Marco's apartment enough?" Maya demanded aloud. She didn't know how close the person who had left the postcard was now. Given that she'd had to approach the door slowly, the person who had delivered the postcard would probably be long gone by now.

Maya still checked the hallway carefully before she bent to pick the postcard up, fearing that some kind of attack might be imminent. When she had it, Maya retreated into her apartment and looked it over.

The design was of one bunny rabbit standing over a hospital bed with another, one whose torso was bandaged and whose face was badly bruised. It took Maya a second to realize that it was meant to be her visiting Marco. Perhaps the Moonlight Killer had just guessed at the scene, but something about the arrangement of it seemed too close to the way things had actually been. He was reminding her that he was watching.

Dear Maya,

I trust that you will take on your next case alone, without the interference of others. Howie Barnet. Chelslake. You have until midnight, two days from now.

*

Maya rushed into the FBI offices with the postcard held in her hand. She needed to get to the office that housed her small task force, although it would just be her and Samit, their tech, now.

She was halfway across the office floor when her boss moved to intercept her.

Agent Harris looked like someone's rich uncle, in a suit that Maya would have struggled to afford, with a golden lapel pin. He was in his fifties, with close cropped salt and pepper hair and a steely expression that didn't have any give in it. Once, Maya might have relied on him to back her up in her cases, giving her the leeway to pursue her work the way she wanted to.

Now, he was almost the opposite.

"Gray, do you want to tell me what the hell is going on?" he demanded. "Detective Spinelli was attacked?"

"That's correct, sir," Maya replied.

"He was shot?"

Again, Maya couldn't deny it. "Yes, sir."

"So this kidnapper whose game you're happily going along with has progressed to trying to kill your partner?"

Maya shook her head, trying to cut off that line of questioning as quickly as she could. "Not trying to kill him. Trying to make sure that he couldn't help me with this case."

"Are you sure about that, Gray?" Harris demanded. "Or is that just what you want to believe?"

"Are you doubting my judgement, sir?"

Harris made a face. He clearly wasn't happy. "I've had doubts about your judgement almost since the start of this, Gray. The fact that this guy has your sister means that you can't be objective about what needs to be done to catch him."

"Meaning throwing ourselves into raids on locations that he's tricked us into going to?" Maya shot back. She had to fight her corner on this. The cold cases the Moonlight Killer sent her out on were hers, and when Harris had tried to run things, he'd only put her sister and the other women in danger.

"This kidnapper has already killed at least one woman, probably two," Harris said, "and now he's showing signs of descending into more erratic behavior. Yet you're running across the office with another postcard in your hand. What is it? Another case from him?"

"One that I will need to solve if I'm going to save a woman's life," Maya pointed out.

"And if I told you that you should spend your time trying to catch him?"

Maya shook her head. It was something that she was planning to do, but not something that she could do to the exclusion of everything else.

"Then I would point out, sir, that I am in charge of my own task force. This is my decision to make."

"For now," Harris shot back. "Until Agent Swift takes it over."

Agent Swift was the head of the task force that was trying to catch the Moonlight Killer. She was driven, determined, and probably just as big a danger to Megan's wellbeing as Harris was.

"Sir?"

"You think no one has noticed that all of the cases this kidnapper is sending you to solve are Moonlight Killer cases?" Harris said. "This is tangled up with the Moonlight Killer hunt, and that means that Swift has every right to claim jurisdiction over it."

He still didn't know the full truth. If he did, he would be shouting by now, or dismissing her outright. He and Swift still hadn't worked out that the kidnapper was the Moonlight Killer, but Maya guessed that it was only a matter of time now.

She had to end this before that happened. She had to get her sister and the others back safely, before Harris charged in with another ill-fated raid. Before that, though, she had to try to solve this case.

"I know you're holding things back, Gray," Harris said. "I know you don't trust me, and frankly, I don't trust you. If I find out that whatever you've been keeping to yourself makes a difference to this case, then I won't just fire you. I'll ensure that the DA looks at charges of obstruction of justice for you."

Maya almost laughed at that. As far as she could tell, she was the only one making any progress toward getting justice on this case, or on any of the cases that the Moonlight Killer sent her to look into.

The only problem was that it wasn't a laughing matter. Harris's threats were serious and dangerous. If he managed to remove her from the case, then her sister was in far more danger than she otherwise might be.

"And with your partner out of action, I want you to take a different one with you. Reyes."

Maya shook her head immediately. Reyes would report back everything Maya did to Harris.

"That's not going to happen sir. This is my task force, and I'm sorry, but I have a case that needs my attention."

One that wouldn't wait for Harris to finish making threats, and which Maya needed information about urgently.

"I'll bear what you said in mind, sir," she said. "For now, though, I have another killer to catch, and I only have two days to do it."

CHAPTER SIX

The town of Chelslake proved to be around a three-hour drive, even with Maya pushing the pace.

It appeared in the distance to her as a spread out, slightly sprawling place, set a little way back from a large lake that stretched into the distance with an island at its heart. There were a few factories and warehouses, but nothing major; Maya guessed that the town brought in most of its income from visitors to the lake. Since it looked a little run down, she guessed that wasn't going as well as the town would have liked.

It occurred to Maya as she approached the town that ordinarily, by this point, she would have had a chance to read through the files from end to end, looking for anything that didn't fit in the original investigation. That, though, was typically because Marco drove when the location was close enough to drive to, giving Maya plenty of time to work. She found herself missing his presence beside her more with each passing mile.

Maya smiled slightly at that. There had been a time when she had been clear to Harris that she neither wanted nor needed a partner, but now, Maya felt almost empty without Marco by her side. She had never imagined that she would reach this point. Or that Marco would come to mean even more to her than that.

Maya would call Marco to make sure that he was ok once she was in town and had started to make some progress on the case. Even then, though, would it be safe to call him?

That thought made Maya pause. The Moonlight Killer had already had Marco shot because he'd been helping too much on the cases. He'd also made it clear that Maya was to do this case alone, and Maya knew that he was listening in to her calls. If he heard her talking to Marco about the case, then was there a chance that he would send someone else to finish Marco?

Maya couldn't risk that. She had to be careful. She couldn't give the Moonlight Killer any reason to think that she was breaking his rules, even as she broke them. Harris and Saoirse had both been right about one thing: the situation was becoming less predictable by the day. Maya needed to find a way to finish this. She needed to find her sister, and the Moonlight Killer.

For now, though, Maya had to focus on the case that she'd been given. If she couldn't get help from Marco, at least she might be able to get information from local law enforcement. With that in mind, her first port of call in Chelslake was the local sheriff's station.

It was a squat, rectangular building in the middle of town with a couple of police cars parked outside. It seemed relatively quiet as Maya walked in, without the usual collection of drunks and petty thieves being brought in for processing that she might have expected at any time of the day if she'd walked into a big city police department.

There was a small reception area there with a deputy staffing a desk. He looked young, and slightly bored, tall and dark-haired, with thin features. He looked up as Maya walked in, and from the sudden spark of interest on his face, she got the impression that there hadn't been much for him to do yet today.

"Can I help you, ma'am?"

Maya showed him her badge. "I was hoping to talk to the sheriff. It's about the Howie Barnet case."

Maya saw the transition from interest to something like shock on the young deputy's features.

"Wait here," he said and rushed for a door at the side of the reception area, disappearing through it for several seconds.

Maya thought she caught hints of a conversation there, just a few fragments of words like "FBI.".

She realized that she should have called ahead, should have gotten Samit to make the arrangements, but after the way things had gone in the office with Harris, she'd felt as though she needed to get on the road as quickly as possible, before Agent Swift had a chance to step in and take her case. Besides, Maya guessed that the Moonlight Killer didn't want Samit helping and she didn't want to put him in the firing line any more than Marco.

It was only a few more seconds before a middle-aged man in a sheriff's uniform came out, giving Maya an obvious appraisal as if trying to work out if she really was who she claimed to be. He was a little shorter than her and slightly overweight, with dark hair that was just starting to gray at the temples.

"I'm Sheriff Lunt. You're the FBI agent?"

Maya held out her badge. "Maya Gray, FBI cold cases unit. I've been sent to look into the death of Howie Barnet."

"Cold?" the sheriff said. "He's barely been dead two months."

If Maya had found a chance to read the file, that was a detail she would have picked up on. As it was, it caught her a little by surprise. Two months was recent, by the standards of the cases the Moonlight Killer was sending her to investigate.

"I've still been sent here to look into it," Maya said.

"Is this as part of that whole Moonlight Killer investigation the FBI has going on?" Sheriff Lunt asked. "We reported it to the FBI because it fit the whole pattern in the press and because... well, you've seen Chelslake. We're a quiet town. We're not equipped to deal with this kind of thing."

"I work for a different team," Maya said. "This case has been linked to a different investigation."

"So *not* the Moonlight Killer?" the sheriff said, sounding both surprised and slightly relieved by it.

"It's unlikely," Maya said. She couldn't explain how she knew that this wasn't a Moonlight Killer case: because the real Moonlight Killer didn't send her to look into his own cases. "But it's still a case I need to try to solve."

The sheriff nodded definitively, clearly happy that Maya was there to take this on and that he didn't have to do it himself. Maya found herself grateful for that, because with so little time, the last thing she needed was hostility from the local PD.

"Can you run me through the details of the case?" Maya asked. "Tell me about the victim and about what happened? I want your take on things."

It would also give her a basic outline of the case until she had time to delve into the details of the case files. With only two days, she had to move quickly.

The sheriff nodded, obviously happy to be able to help. "The victim was Howie Barnet, 27, lived locally. He went out to the lake, and our initial investigation suggests that he was lured there by the promise of a romantic encounter with a woman. Turned out that Howie was something of a lothario, had a lot of girlfriends. We looked at that angle, but there didn't seem to be anything there, and the method of the killing... strangulation under the full moon..."

"It seemed so close to the Moonlight Killer's MO that it had to be him?" Maya guessed. She'd heard that before on cases. The local PD saw what looked like the Moonlight Killer and because of that they stopped looking deeper. They thought that they had an answer, and so they didn't keep looking for other options.

The sheriff looked a little worried then, as if he was sure that there was going to be trouble coming from that. "Yeah, I guess."

"I want to look at other options," Maya said. "Tell me more about Howie Barnet. Who was he? What did he do for a living?"

"His day job was in some marketing firm," Sheriff Lunt said. "We have a couple here in town that have worked out that it's easier to base themselves somewhere smaller and occasionally travel into the big cities than to pay real estate prices in D.C."

"Were there any problems with any of his clients?" Maya asked. "Any troubles at work with his colleagues?"

"None that we saw." The sheriff sounded confident in that. It seemed like he'd checked at least a few things before deciding that it was the Moonlight Killer.

"Tell me more about the spot where he was killed." Maya said.

"That was out on the island," the sheriff replied. "There's an island in the middle of the lake that has become kind of a tourist attraction. The guy who used to own it decided that he wanted to make it into a place for people to come. He paid a lot of local artists to leave works out there in the trees, and even had this big, ruined tower built. It gave the town something it could use to attract visitors."

"And he was over there to meet with a woman?" Maya said.

"Or he thought he was." Sheriff Lunt shrugged. "We checked, and the woman who messaged him doesn't even exist. It's a stock photograph and an account made using an anonymous email."

A trap, in other words, although one that was interesting in its way, because it raised the question of whether it was there to lure in any man it could, or whether it was aimed specifically at the victim in this case.

"So he was strangled there on the island?" Maya said.

"Right on the shoreline near the tower, strangled from behind with a rope and left there."

Maya could see why the local PD had thought that this might be the work of the Moonlight Killer. This was one of the cases where the similarities in MO were closer to the original, one that even Maya might have taken as his work at first glance if she didn't know better.

She considered her next moves. She needed to get more of a sense of how the murder had happened, then go from there. That left her with one obvious next move.

"I think I need to take a look at this island to see the spot where the murder took place," Maya said.

"I'll take you out there if you like," the sheriff offered.

Maya almost accepted automatically. After all, the sheriff would know the spot well and would be able to direct her to it, as well as being able to talk her through the way the initial investigation on the scene had gone. It seemed obvious that she should go with him.

Then she thought of Marco and what had happened to him. It was enough to make Maya hesitate. Would the Moonlight Killer view it as breaking his rules if Maya took the local sheriff with her on this case? She knew that she couldn't risk it, both for his safety and that of her sister.

"It's all right," Maya said. "I'll find it. I prefer to work alone."

Once, that had been true, but now, it was a necessity to try to keep anyone else from getting hurt in the course of the Moonlight Killer's deadly game.

"If you're sure?" Sheriff Lunt said.

Maya nodded. "I'm not going to take you away from your duties just to escort me around. Thank you for your help."

Maya moved toward the door. If there wasn't anything else to learn here, she didn't have any time to waste. She had to get to the island before her deadline ran out.

CHAPTER SEVEN

Maya parked close to the lake, looking out toward the island, and trying to imagine what it would have been like for Howie Barnet as he arrived. It was hard to do when it seemed that plenty of the inhabitants of Chelslake and probably a lot of tourists had all decided today that they wanted to be down by the lake.

The whole place was bright and bustling in a way it wouldn't have been at night, with several stores in shacks down by the water selling everything from food and drinks to tourist trinkets. There were couples strolling along the shoreline, groups of kids playing, and several boats out on the water.

Maya got out her phone and finally pulled up the case files as she looked out at the island. The coroner's report was there, confirming that the cause of death was strangulation, with no additional elements to suggest a different MO beyond a simple surprise attack. Howie had a couple of bruises on his knuckles, suggesting that he'd struck out at his attacker, but the coroner hadn't been able to recover DNA evidence.

The report on the crime scene was a little more interesting, showing images of the way the place had been set up for a romantic encounter. It seemed as if the killer had wanted Howie in one particular spot, right by the water. Maya found herself wondering if that was because it was the best spot to ambush someone or if there had been another reason for it.

Maya knew that the only way to know for sure would be to make her way over to the island.

She got out of the car, doing her best to retrace Howie's steps as far as the crime scene report had been able to establish them. His car had been found abandoned in the morning by one of the crew who cleaned up and looked after the area around the shoreline. That car had been roughly… there, if Maya was able to judge the positioning in the photograph correctly. Fragments of paper had been found nailed to a post *here*, suggesting a message had been left for him.

Maya looked out toward the shoreline. There were several boats tied up there. One of them looked just about ready to leave, with a few tourists aboard, obviously heading to the island. Maya joined them, continuing to read as she went, while trying to make sure that no one else saw any images in the file that would disturb them. A rowboat had been found near the shore. Maya tried to imagine Howie crossing this stretch of water, thinking that there was a woman waiting for him at the end of it all.

Why the island? Maya found herself looking back toward the shore as she asked that question. It was busy now, but presumably it had been deserted that night. Had the killer just not been willing to take the risk of someone coming by unexpectedly? Or did the island have some significance for them?

The boat pulled up to the island and Maya leapt ashore, again very aware that she only had today and tomorrow in which to work on this case. She hurried across the island, trying to follow the tourist trails to find the spot where the murder had taken place. Thankfully, the constant presence of the tower in the distance meant that she could make quick progress in the right direction.

She took twists and turns until she came out into an open space that contained the ruined tower. There were tourists moving around it, taking pictures, or just exploring the structure that was built to look ruined from the very start.

Maya's interest was in the cover it might have provided to a killer. Had the killer waited there to ambush Howie? If so, why lure him all the way to the edge of the water?

That was one part of this that didn't make sense. As far as Maya could tell, there had been plenty of spots for an ambush all the way across the island, and in some of them, the body wouldn't have been found as quickly. Maybe the killer didn't care about that, or even wanted Howie to be found; but still, why *here*?

Maya could only assume that the spot was significant in some way. She walked up to it, using crime scene photographs to try to get a sense of exactly where it had been. She thought she had it after a few minutes, thought that she was standing in exactly the spot that Howie would have been when he died.

As far as Maya could tell, there was nothing special about it. It offered a view back out over the lake towards the shore, but that was it. Was there something more to it that she didn't understand?

There was no way to tell, and it seemed obvious to her now that she wasn't going to get much from being here on the island. Maya knew that she could keep looking around, but she simply didn't have enough time. She needed to try something else that might help jump-start the investigation.

Maybe talking to Howie Barnet's family would help to give her something she could work with. She looked for the number in the case file for Howie's next of kin, ready to make a call to arrange a visit.

*

To Maya, the home of Lyle Barnet looked like a typical suburban house, the kind of place that might have been bought with a family in mind. It sat in the middle of a neat row of other houses, a sedan sitting on the driveway. Even as Maya went up to knock on the door, it opened, revealing a man who had to be Howie's brother.

Lyle Barnet didn't look much like his sibling. He was probably only a few years older, but his features were less youthful looking, partly obscured by a full dark beard. His hair hung loose down to his shoulders, while he wore round spectacles. He was currently wearing a suit.

"Agent Gray?"

Maya nodded. "Mr. Barnet? Thank you for meeting me like this."

"Please come in. Can we do this quick? I have to be back at the office soon."

Maya had as much desire as Howie's brother to work quickly, given her own time constraints, but she still wanted to find out as much as possible. Any information she could get might help to point her in the right direction.

She followed him into the house, into a small study filled with architectural drawings. Lyle Barnet took a seat on one side of a broad oak desk dominated by a computer monitor. Maya took a seat opposite him.

"What has prompted you to come look into my brother's murder like this, Agent Gray?"

"You don't want me to find the man who did this?" Maya countered, slightly surprised.

"Of course I do! I'm just surprised that you're here. The local sheriff's department handed all of this over to the FBI, and then we've heard nothing since. Why now?"

Maya couldn't give him the real reason. At least not all of it. "I work cold cases. This one came to my attention through another investigation. But I need to know as much as possible about your brother's life."

"What do you want to know?" Lyle asked. He seemed a little less confrontational now that he was sure that Maya was committed to solving his brother's case.

Maya started with the basics. "Can you think of anyone who had a reason to hurt him?"

"The police already asked me that," Lyle replied.

"And my guess is that after they left, you started to ask yourself if there *might* have been anyone," Maya said. "As I said, I work cold cases. I know that with time, people sometimes think of things that didn't occur to them earlier, or that have only started to make sense as time has passed."

Lyle still shook his head, though. "Howie worked in marketing. He didn't make enemies. He made friends."

"With women?" Maya asked.

"What do you mean?"

"As I understand it, your brother was lured to the island with the promise of a romantic liaison. Was that a common thing for him?"

Maya saw Lyle hesitate slightly, then nod.

"There were… a lot of women in his life. Howie was never really the kind of guy to settle with someone."

"A lot of one-night stands?" Maya said.

Lyle nodded again.

Maya couldn't see someone killing him over a one-night stand, though. Not unless things had gone particularly badly. If he were a predator and this was some kind of punishment for that, Maya might expect there to be some hint of that somewhere. She would have expected that the sheriff's people would have picked up on it.

"Was there anyone he was with for longer?" Maya asked.

Lyle looked uncomfortable then, and just that look of discomfort caught her interest.

"What is it?" she asked.

"There was one woman. Olivia. He'd been seeing her off and on for a while. Normally, he was happy to talk about the women in his life, but this one… he was kind of secretive about her. I got the feeling that things didn't end that well."

"What makes you say that?" Maya asked, her interest caught. A woman he'd been in a more serious relationship with, and then broken up with, might have been angry. Angry enough to do something like this?

"I got the feeling that she wasn't happy that he kept seeing other women," Lyle said.

Which perhaps made the whole fake romantic encounter make sense. Maybe this woman had decided that it was the best kind of justice to exact against him for what he had done.

"Look, I'm sorry," Lyle said, "but it sounds like you're not looking at anything new, and I really do have to go back to work."

He clearly didn't believe that Maya was going to make much progress in the case. Maya considered pressing him for more, but suspected that if he knew anything, he would have mentioned it.

"All right," Maya said. She pushed over one of her cards. "But if you think of anything that might be relevant, no matter how small it seems, please contact me."

She left, heading back to her car. There, she looked over the files on her phone again, looking for references to this woman: Olivia. She quickly found a reference to Olivia Jones, married to Ernest Jones. The original investigation had briefly looked at her, with the sheriff questioning her, then clearing her because she'd been out of town that night.

She had an alibi, which meant that this was a dead end. She needed to think of something else. At this point in a case, Maya might have talked things over with Marco, but she knew that simply calling him would put him in danger.

She needed to find another way.

CHAPTER EIGHT

He sat in front of his computer, hating himself. Hating what he was, hating what he did. That wasn't going to stop him from doing it, though. If a compulsion were that easy to stop then it wouldn't be a compulsion.

The room around him was gloomy even in the daytime, the blinds closed to shut out the light. His fingers, too stubby, too fat, clattered against the keyboard of his laptop as he chatted in another man's private messages.

Thanks for the compliments. Maybe we should meet up.

Of course, the photograph wasn't of him. That wouldn't have attracted any of the attention that he was currently getting. Instead, he'd picked a stock photograph of a pretty young woman, using a different account from last time. This one, he'd called Izzie.

That's pretty quick, his target replied. Benjamin Malt was a grad-student, a smart guy. Yet he was sure that even smart guys could be brought to the right spot at the right time if he could only find the correct words to do so.

Well, I'm a girl who likes to work quickly. When I see something I want, I go for it. Don't you?

There was a pause as Benjamin Malt typed. For a few seconds, the man pretending to be Izzie wondered if he'd pushed too far, too fast. But he'd seen Malt's profile and his posts. He was a man who talked about going out and grabbing life by the throat, seizing the moment.

In this specific context, they were both sentiments that the man typing could definitely get behind. Although it wasn't *life's* throat he was interested in.

Finally, Benjamin Malt replied.

Yes, I like to go for what I want when I see it. And when I see you, I want you.

That brought a flicker of relief. The right photograph, the right words, could achieve anything. Or at least, they could get men to the places where he could kill them.

Again, he felt a flicker of disgust with himself at the things he did, at the things he was. If people saw him the way he saw himself, they would never go near him. He was disgusting, something the world would be better off without.

But then, so were the men he killed. They deserved to die. There was even a brief, flickering satisfaction as he killed them, which was only replaced afterwards by still greater disgust, and the need to find another to reduce that feeling.

That's good to hear, he replied to Malt. *Maybe we could meet up tonight?*

My place? Malt replied.

That didn't work. He would never get past the front door. Malt would see that he wasn't who he claimed to be and know instantly that this was about something more dangerous than a simple hookup. No, he had to draw the other man out, bring him to a location that he could control. Somewhere out in the open, somewhere with all the elements that he required for this.

Is it wrong that I get a thrill out of hooking up outdoors?

A simple ploy, one that had worked before.

Are you sure you wouldn't prefer somewhere warmer? Malt countered.

I'll bring a blanket. Come on, where's your sense of adventure? Outdoors, under the stars.

There was a pause long enough that it was frustrating. Had he lost Malt in spite of all his efforts? Was he going to have to try to ambush him some other way? He hated himself for the failure, as well as for everything else.

I'm not sure I can do it tonight, Malt replied. *Maybe it's better to meet up in the daytime? Get to know one another a little?*

Was he just getting cold feet, or was he suspicious? And daylight? That would make his approach harder. He worked better at night, when no one could see him. Either way, the man typing could work with it. He had to.

That's fine. It means I get to see you better. Tomorrow?

Tomorrow works for me.

But I get to pick the place, ok? I know the perfect *spot.*

CHAPTER NINE

The first thing Maya did was find a spot where she could buy a burner phone, paying for it in cash and walking to the store where she bought it from several blocks away. She doubted that the Moonlight Killer would be tracking her car or her credit card transactions, but Maya wasn't about to take the chance.

The second thing she did was to call Marco on her normal phone. It would look suspicious if she didn't call him at all, and that suspicion could be just as dangerous as if she came out and started asking him for help on the case.

He answered quickly. "Maya, where are you?"

"I'm out on a case," Maya said. "I'm just calling to see how you're doing."

"You're on a case without me? Alone?" Marco sounded suddenly worried.

"It's what the Moonlight Killer's insisting on," Maya said.

"So he's trying to get you out there alone? Have you considered the possibility that he's doing it so that he can target you?"

Again, Maya could hear the worry in his voice, only growing as the conversation went on. She could understand that worry. Maybe the Moonlight Killer *was* trying to lure her somewhere alone because he'd tired of his game. That was a terrifying thought, particularly because Maya had to keep going even then.

"I don't have a choice, Marco. It's his game, and I have to play by his rules."

"So he has complete control of the situation?"

"I just have to find the answers here. I can do it. I was just calling to check that you're doing better."

"I'm fine," Marco said. "I'll be out of the hospital in a few days. Now, tell me about the case."

Maya had guessed he would say that, and she knew what she had to say in return. "I don't think I can do that, Marco. It would still be you helping me. We can't risk it."

"Maya-"

"I have to go. I'm sorry."

Maya hung up and headed back to the car. She put her phone in it, then walked a little way away, took out her burner phone and punched in Marco's number. Even this was a small risk, because Maya knew that the Moonlight Killer had the capacity to look through security cameras, but she didn't think that he would intercept random calls coming in to Marco's phone.

"Hello?" Marco said.

"Marco, it's me. I'm calling from a different phone because he'll be listening in on my main one. We'll have to be quick. This has to look like just someone else calling to check on how you're doing."

"I understand," Marco said, "but what are you doing out there, Maya?"

"My job. I have to solve this case if I'm going to save another woman's life."

Maya heard Marco sigh, but he seemed to get the message that she wasn't suddenly going to walk away from a case.

"Does this phone mean that you can talk about the case now?" he asked.

"If we're quick. There seems to be one victim so far: Howie Barnet, strangled at night after being lured to an island by someone who made him think he was meeting a woman."

"The local PD wrote it off as the Moonlight Killer?" Marco asked.

"Yes, but they seem to have asked some of the basic questions. I briefly thought there might be something, but it turned out that they'd already looked at it."

"What kind of something?" Marco asked.

"Howie Barnet had plenty of one-night stands and brief relationships, but there was one woman, Olivia Jones, who his brother said he had an on again, off again relationship with. One Howie was secretive about. But like I said, the local PD looked at her. She had an alibi."

"What about a husband or a boyfriend?" Marco asked.

"What?" It occurred to Maya then that she hadn't thought the situation through, and just taken the sheriff department's assessment of the situation at face value.

"Well, why was he being so secretive about the relationship if there wasn't someone like that around?" Marco pointed out. "Either there's going to be a husband somewhere, or, if there isn't, there must be some reason he was being so secretive."

"You're right." It was obvious now that they'd had a chance to talk about it. In that moment, Maya remembered why she'd grown to like having Marco around as a partner and how much she'd come to rely on him.

Of course, in her personal life, she liked having him around for plenty of other reasons too.

"I have to go," she said. "I only have until midnight tomorrow. Just concentrate on getting better, okay?"

"And *you* watch your back. I still think that there's a reason why the Moonlight Killer has tried to isolate you on this one."

Maya hung up, hoping that Marco was wrong about that part. She tucked away the burner phone and went back to her car. When she got there, she saw that there had been a call to her main phone, from Agent Swift.

Maya braced herself and called back.

"Agent Gray," Agent Swift said as she picked up. "Would you mind telling me what's going on?"

"What do you mean?"

"Don't try playing stupid," the senior agent snapped. "I want to know why you're looking into another Moonlight Killer case."

Maya swallowed, trying to work out what options she had before she answered. She also knew that she couldn't hesitate now, though, because that would only make Agent Swift more suspicious.

Maya tried the variation of the truth that she'd told to Harris in the past.

"The kidnapper in the case I'm working is the one who picks out the cold cases for me to look at. If they're connected to the Moonlight Killer, that just reflects his obsessions."

"Or your own."

"Agent Swift-"

"Every case you've looked into since this began has had something to do with the Moonlight Killer."

"*None* of them have," Maya corrected the other agent. "Agent Swift, it may look like I'm treading on your toes with these investigations, but every one of them so far has proven to be committed by someone else."

It was the only card she had left to play right then, the only way of making sure that she got to keep her autonomy in all of this. The moment Agent Swift could prove that this was all about the Moonlight Killer, the case fell under her task force, not Maya's.

"And how did someone know that?" Agent Swift asked.

It was a question that made Maya's blood run cold. It was the question that had led her to work out that this was all down to the Moonlight Killer, so she had no doubt that, given enough time, Agent Swift would work out the same thing.

"I'm working on the theory that this is someone who is particularly good at deducing things, who may even have worked out the truth of each of the cases," Maya said. Again, it was close to the truth. A part of her *was* convinced that the Moonlight Killer had worked out the truth of at least some of the cases before she had.

"Then why send you after these people like this?" Agent Swift asked. "That doesn't make sense. They could just phone in tips to the FBI. Why would someone bother kidnapping a group of women to force you to investigate these cases?"

"I'll be sure to ask him that when I catch up to him," Maya said. "All I know is that I have a psychopath sending me out to solve cases, and with this one, I only have until midnight tomorrow. I'm sorry, Agent Swift, but I don't have time to argue about whose task force this should fall under. If you have any further concerns, I'll do my best to address them, but for now, I really need to go."

Maya hung up, leaning against the side of her car, and breathing hard. She found herself hoping that she'd gotten away with it. She hadn't, though, she was sure of it. Not long term.

That one slip she'd made had been crucial. Agent Swift wasn't stupid, as she'd proven the moment she'd picked up on the question of how the kidnapper knew that these weren't real Moonlight Killer cases. Add to that the fact that Agent Harris already had suspicions about Maya. If the two talked, eventually, they would come to the conclusion that Maya was holding back the Moonlight Killer's involvement in all of this. They would realize that ultimately, only the Moonlight Killer knew which kills had been down to him and which were done by other people.

It was another layer of pressure in an already difficult case. Maya found herself staring at her phone, wondering if the Moonlight Killer had been listening in to all of that. Would he be laughing to himself at the trouble Maya was going to be in over all of this? Would he be enjoying the increasing pressure on Maya?

Or would he be angry that things were falling apart? Would he lash out if she lost control of the case, particularly if she wasn't allowed to keep working on it? Might he view it as a breach of his game? Might he even decide to cut his losses by killing his remaining captives?

Maya had to do everything she could to stop that from happening.

For now, that meant trying to solve this case. It meant Maya using public records to try to find information on Olivia Jones.

It didn't take her long to find that Olivia Jones had a husband, Alvin Jones, but that she had recently divorced from him. That seemed like a telling detail. It was possible that it had happened because the affair had come out in the investigation, but what if he'd found out earlier than that? What if he'd learned that his wife was sleeping with Howie Barnet and decided to kill him? What if he'd decided that the best way to deal with the situation was to strangle him and make it look like the work of the Moonlight Killer?

Maya didn't know if that was what had happened, but it was an angle that no one else had looked into so far. That meant there was at least a chance it would help her to find the killer.

It also meant that she needed to find Alvin Jones right away.

CHAPTER TEN

It was getting dark as Maya pulled up outside Alvin Jones's home address. Between the time it had taken to get to the town, her trip to the island, and the time she'd spent speaking with Lyle Barnet, she'd already used up most of her first, precious day.

There was a car on the driveway of the small family house. That was good. Maya didn't want to have to use up any more time running around looking for Alvin's workplace or even waiting for him.

Maya took in the house for a moment as she sat there, particularly the for sale sign out front. Did Alvin have to sell up because of the divorce? If so, Maya guessed that it would only add to a sense of him losing everything, a sense that might have given him all the reason he needed to kill.

Maya strode up to the door, watching carefully for any sign of someone trying to run, or that she was about to come under attack. That had happened before, approaching suspects' houses with Marco, but in those situations at least she'd always known that she had him to back her up. She was back to being alone, and that meant that Maya had to watch for all the potential dangers of the situation herself.

The man who answered the door was a little taller than Maya, dark-haired, in his early thirties, with slightly rounded features and wide-set gray eyes.

"Yes, who are you?" he asked.

"Alvin Jones? I'm Agent Gray, with the FBI."

"The FBI?"

"This is about the murder of Howie Barnet." As Maya said his name, she watched Alvin's face, trying to pick up his reactions." I need to ask you some questions."

Maya saw worry there, but also a note of confusion, as if Alvin couldn't quite understand why Maya was there.

"You want to question *me*?" he said. "I'm not sure that I know anything about all of it. I certainly don't want to talk about Howie Barnet."

"May I come in?" Maya asked.

She saw him hesitate. His reluctance was starting to make her a little more suspicious.

"Mr. Jones," Maya said. "There are some issues around Howie Barnet's death that we need to clear up. We can do it at the door if you want, but it may be easier inside."

"I'm fine here," Alvin said. He was leaning against the door, one hand on it, like he was getting ready to shut it as quickly as possible once they were done. He clearly didn't want Maya there.

"All right," Maya said. "Tell me about your ex-wife."

Alvin made a face then, a mixture of anger and sadness crossing his features at once.

"You think that I want to talk about Olivia?"

Maya knew that this wasn't about what he wanted, it was about what he'd potentially done.

"I think it might be relevant to my case," she said. "Why did you break up?"

"What business is that of the FBI's?" Alvin asked.

Maya was starting to lose patience with him, so she decided to set it all out clearly for him.

"Let's put this simply, Mr. Jones. Around the time of his murder, Howie Barnet was having an affair with your wife. There are plenty of people who would say that would give you a good reason to be angry, that you had a strong motive for murder."

She saw Alvin's eyes widen in surprise at that.

"You think that I killed him?"

Maya stared at him levelly, trying to convey just how serious she was about all of this.

"I don't know, Mr. Jones. Did you?"

"Of course I didn't!" Alvin said. He started to close the door. Maya put a hand against it.

"We can have this conversation down at the sheriff's office if you'd prefer, but we *are* going to have it."

She didn't have enough time to deal with a guy who was refusing to cooperate like this.

"Agent, as I understand it, I don't have to answer your questions. If you think you have enough evidence to arrest me, do it, but I didn't have anything to do with Howie Barnet's murder."

He made to shut the door again and Maya had a split second to decide what she was going to do. Her first instinct was to push the door open, put cuffs on him, and question him down at the sheriff's office. Maya knew that she didn't have enough to do that, though; a potential motive wasn't enough without some physical evidence to back it up.

Maya had to let him shut the door, going back to her car, and backing away a little from the house. She considered driving straight back to the sheriff's station, trying to find another way to go on this case.

Instead, though, Maya waited. There had been something very off about the way Alvin had been determined to get rid of her. Maybe it was just that he didn't want to be caught up in a murder investigation, but Maya had the feeling that there was more to it than that. That was why she waited and, when Alvin came out of the house a few minutes later, getting in his car and driving off, she followed him.

Ordinarily, when the FBI followed someone, it involved a mixture of surveillance techniques. A whole team would be involved, using drones and traffic cameras to keep a suspect in sight, trading off between themselves so that no one person would be behind the suspect for too long. Often, using a team meant that it was even possible to follow a suspect from in front, switching off to new agents every time they took a turn, then reacquiring them later.

Maya didn't have the backup to make an approach like that work, so she had to settle for hanging back from Alvin Jones's car, driving as normally as possible, and simply hoping that he wouldn't spot her.

Maya had experience in following people without the full backup of a team from her military days. The trick was not to do anything to draw attention to herself, and not to match the suspect's vehicle too exactly. Drivers picked up on someone speeding up and slowing down every time they did. It was better to let them get a little ahead and reel them in, like an angler playing out fishing line.

Maya kept Alvin's vehicle in sight, following through the twists and turns of the town, making sure that she never got close enough to spook him. When he stopped outside an apartment block, Maya drove past and then pulled up, running back to follow him in. She was in time to see him entering an elevator, and saw it stop on the third floor.

Maya found a stairwell and ran up the stairs as fast as she could. There was a risk, now that Alvin had broken line of sight with her, that he might simply disappear. Maya couldn't allow that to happen. She sprinted up to the third floor and came out onto a landing in time to see Alvin heading into an apartment.

Maya considered pausing, considered listening at the door, yet she had the same feeling that she'd had throughout this case: that she was running short of time. She needed to know what was going on here, so she went over to that apartment and knocked on the door. It opened a few moments later, revealing a woman in her twenties, with straight blonde hair, blue eyes, and high cheekbones. She was wearing jeans and a pale sweater.

"Yes, can I help you?" she said.

Maya held up her badge. "I'm here to see Alvin."

At the sound of her voice, Alvin came to the door from the interior of the apartment. He looked at Maya with obvious fear, as if she'd just discovered some great secret.

"You? You can't be here! Did you follow me?"

"Yes," Maya said simply. "With how spooked you seemed back at your place, I wanted to know what was going on."

"I..." Alvin hesitated, obviously wondering if he should try to shut this door on Maya too.

"Alvin, what's going on?" the woman at the door demanded. "Why is the FBI here?"

"It's ok, Candice," Alvin said. He looked over to Maya and sighed. "You're not going to give up, are you? Ok, you'd better come in. I can explain things. Candice, let her in."

Maya went through into an ordinary looking apartment, where she took a seat on a dark leather couch. She looked over at Alvin expectantly.

"Ok, Alvin, I'm listening," Maya said. "What had you so spooked back at the house?"

"It... it's my divorce," Alvin said. "You see, Agent Gray, before Olivia cheated on me with... that man, I had already been seeing Candice here. Olivia and I were separated at the time of Howie Barnet's death."

"That doesn't explain the secrecy or the defensiveness," Maya said.

"You saw the realtor's sign outside my house?" Alvin demanded. "Olivia's lawyers are trying to take me for everything I have, but they don't have as much information as they would like so far."

“So you’re worried that if you answer too many questions in my investigation, it all ends up as part of the public record, and they use it against you?” Maya guessed.

“I… yes. I didn’t want them knowing that I’m still seeing Candice. Olivia will find a way to make me pay for that. The divorce is going badly enough; I don’t want to make things worse.”

“The quickest way to ensure that everything gets written down is to keep refusing to cooperate,” Maya said. “I’m not interested in your marriage, Mr. Jones. I just want to establish if you had any involvement in Howie Barnet’s murder.”

Alvin shook his head sharply. “I told you before, I didn’t have anything to do with it. I didn’t care about him. I wasn’t angry with him for sleeping with Olivia. If I was angry with anyone, then, it was with myself.”

If that was true, then he wouldn’t have as much of a motive as Maya had thought for the murder. Still, she wanted to check now that she finally had him answering questions.

“Do you remember where you were the night of Howie Barnet’s murder?” she asked.

Alvin shook his head, though. “It was two months ago. I don’t remember where I was. I certainly couldn’t prove it if I did.”

Meaning that he had no alibi, but then, most people wouldn’t be able to supply an alibi that far back, not unless they happened to go out somewhere special or take a trip that day.

It wasn’t enough to bring Alvin in, not without any corroborating evidence to tie him to the scene.

“Can you think of anyone else who might have had a reason to hurt Howie Barnet?” Maya asked him. “Did Olivia say anything about him that you think might be relevant?”

He shook his head, though. “He’s just not a guy I knew anything about, except to find out that he was sleeping with Olivia. I didn’t care about him at the time, and I haven’t given him a lot of thought since. Until you showed up at my door, I figured he didn’t have anything to do with me.”

Candice cut in then, putting a hand on Alvin’s shoulder. “Do you have what you need from us now?”

Maya nodded. This wasn’t going anywhere. She got up to leave.

“Thank you for your time.”

Maya headed back down to her car and used her laptop to look into Alvin Jones on the FBI's systems. He didn't have a criminal record that she could find, nothing to suggest a history of violence. A look at Howie Barnet's social media didn't show any messages from him.

It seemed he was telling the truth in that respect: Howie simply hadn't mattered to him.

Although he would stay on Maya's list of suspects, she was increasingly getting the feeling that he didn't have anything to do with this. She needed to look in a new direction, and finding that new direction meant that she needed to head back to the sheriff's office.

CHAPTER ELEVEN

It was getting late, but Maya sat at a desk in one corner of the sheriff's office, looking through the sheriff's paper copies of the case files and trying to find something, anything that would let her look at the case from a fresh angle.

"What are you looking for in there?" Sheriff Lunt asked.

That was the problem; Maya didn't know. She was just hoping that there would be *something*. Anything that would let her get closer to an answer in all of this.

"I'll know it when I see it," Maya said. "Anything that stands out, anything that gives me a way into this case."

"I don't know what you're going to find in the files," Sheriff Lunt said. "I helped to write them, remember? We did all the standard things. There just wasn't a lot to look at on the case."

"There was Olivia Jones's ex-husband," Maya pointed out. "There's still a chance that he could have been angry at her sleeping with Howie Barnet."

"But you don't believe that," Sheriff Lunt said. "Or you would have brought him in."

"I don't have any physical evidence linking him to the crimes." Maya shook her head. "I need any evidence I can find. Whoever did this, we either need direct physical evidence or we need to understand the crime to the point where the why and the how can lead us to the who."

She saw the sheriff shrug. "Our forensics couldn't pull much from the scene. There wasn't any DNA on the rope used in the strangulation, none of the things used to set up the romantic scene had any prints, the island doesn't have any security cameras. I just don't think that there's any physical evidence to find."

Maya was more determined than that, though.

"There will be something. There must be. I wouldn't have been sent here if there weren't some way into this case."

She had to believe that. The Moonlight Killer hadn't sent her to investigate an impossible case so far. There had always been a way to get to the truth, however difficult it proved. Occasionally, he'd even sent her clues to help get her onto the right track.

Maya could have used one of those clues now, but she didn't think that she was going to get one. Things with the Moonlight Killer were starting to break down. The situation was becoming more chaotic.

"Why don't you call it a night?" Sheriff Lunt suggested. "Start again in the morning?"

Maya shook her head. She couldn't stop, not now. She only had until tomorrow night. She couldn't just walk away from the case for the night, couldn't just go to a hotel and rest when any moment might be the one when she came up with an answer.

"I need to keep going."

"You sound like you want to solve it all today," Sheriff Lunt said, sounding like he didn't understand. Of course, he couldn't, and Maya couldn't explain the reasons why she needed to solve the case by tomorrow night without giving away far too much about the situation.

That reminded her of the first case she'd worked in this ordeal, following the trail of that first postcard, not even able to tell Marco about what was happening at first. It had just been Maya, trying to get to the truth of a case, trying to feel her way through the lies to get to the truth.

"I don't have long here," Maya said. "I get sent in for brief windows to investigate. If I can't make a breakthrough quickly, I'll be pulled out."

And a woman would be dead. Maya couldn't allow that to happen.

"Well, you can keep going here as long as you want to," Sheriff Lunt said. "Personally, I'm going home to get some sleep, but there will be at least a couple of deputies around all night if you need anything."

"Thank you," Maya said, then watched him leave. What she mostly needed was some kind of inspiration in this case.

Maya sat there, trying to think of possible ways to get closer to the killer. Trying to understand him. What did he want in all of this? Why had he committed the murder in the precise way that he had?

It was tempting to think that he'd chosen to strangle his victim under a full moon purely because it would disguise the crime as a Moonlight Killer murder. Maya wasn't sure she believed that, though.

Not entirely. A killer trying to do that wouldn't have lured his victims by using a method that the real Moonlight Killer hadn't bothered with. *He* seemed to just stalk his victims, picking his moment somewhere within their daily life.

The strangulation might have been picked for convenience, but Maya felt that there was always something personal about it, something that meant being closer to a victim for longer than with any other method.

That could mean that the killer took pleasure in it, or simply that he hated his victims so much that he wanted to savor the moment of their deaths. If it were something simple, something random, why not just shoot Howie? Yet shouldn't such hatred be obvious somewhere else? Wouldn't there be signs of it online?

Maya started to search Howie Barnet's social media profiles, looking for anyone who had sent him messages declaring their hate or wishing him dead. There was nothing obvious there. No one had threatened him. No one had shown the kind of hatred that would lead someone to kill that close.

Maya looked at Howie's business affairs next. Was there anything there that might have led to him being a target? If there were, then surely there would be some hint of scandal relating to that work? Some sign that he was in trouble? Samit had sent across copies of his emails, and there was nothing in there to indicate a client out for blood, willing to disguise it all as the Moonlight Killer's work.

Maya pinched the bridge of her nose. She was getting tired now. Maybe she should have gone to find somewhere to stay, but she had only a little more than 24 hours left. Maya couldn't imagine completing a full investigation in that time from where she was, but she didn't have any other choice.

She got up for a few seconds, walking around the office and trying to stretch. She needed to think about something, anything, other than the case for a few minutes. Maya considered calling Marco just to hear his voice, but she wasn't sure if it was a good idea. It was getting late, and he would probably only tell her that she needed to stop for the night. Besides, if she called him too often, there was a chance that the Moonlight Killer would assume that they were trying to circumvent his restrictions. Since that was exactly what Maya was doing with the burner phone, she didn't dare risk it.

Instead, she used the sheriff's computer to go online and start looking again at rashes caused by poisonous plants. It was something Maya didn't want to do on her phone because there was a good chance that he would see whatever she used it to look at, but it was something she couldn't give up on.

Maya wasn't like Harris and Reyes, charging off after every hint of the location in which the Moonlight Killer was holding the women, but if she could get a real location for him, if she could find where her sister was, then she could end all of this.

It was slow going. As Maya had seen before, pictures of such rashes often weren't well categorized, meaning that she had to scroll through them, simply hoping that there would be something that matched up with the rash she remembered on Saoirse's arm.

Then Maya hit the jackpot, in the form of a website dedicated to identifying what hikers might have been stung, bitten, or poisoned by. There were whole pages dedicated to different types of wasps, flies, and fungi, but Maya wasn't interested in those. She clicked straight through to a page dedicated to plants with contact poison qualities that produced rashes.

Each plant had a brief description along with a picture of the rash it produced. It was exactly the kind of thing that Maya was looking for, and that might save her a lot of time. She started to look through the listings, trying to find one that looked correct.

When she saw the one that matched, Maya felt a wave of excitement running through her. Poison Sumac. *That* was what had caused the rash on Saoirse's arm. Was that helpful, though? The site said that it was relatively common in the areas where it was found…

Except that West Virginia wasn't listed as one of those areas.

Maya searched for the plant in conjunction with the state and found that it was very rare there. So rare that it was just a few pockets, typically in relatively isolated places. If Maya could find those pockets, then she might have a genuine chance of cross referencing them with the saw-whet owl to find the location where the Moonlight Killer was keeping the women.

The only question now was how Maya was meant to go about doing that. There didn't seem to be any convenient maps of the locations of the plant, which meant that she couldn't simply lay one over the other. She needed to find an expert.

That would be a job for tomorrow. No expert would still be awake, let alone at work, right now. Besides, Maya needed to keep going with the case. She couldn't bet everything on being able to find the Moonlight Killer's bunker in time. She had to find an answer in this case.

Maya went back to looking through the files, trying to decide if perhaps the location was significant. Was the island special to the killer? It seemed that he'd lured Howie to that one specific spot to kill him, so there had to be a reason for that. Did Howie Barnet have any particular connection to the island that might explain it?

Maya started looking back through his social media, trying to find an answer. She could feel her eyelids growing heavy as she did, feeling it become increasingly difficult to stare at the screen. Maybe she'd overestimated how easy it would be to keep going through the night with all of this. She needed some rest.

All right. One quick nap. Maya leaned back in the sheriff's chair. She would be awake again in an hour, ready to keep going, trying to find an answer. The answers were there somewhere, but she couldn't see them when she was so tired. One brief rest, and she would get right back to it.

CHAPTER TWELVE

Maya had done it. She'd found the place. Between the details of the saw-whet owl's habitat and the poison sumac, Maya had narrowed it down to one cabin, in one clearing. The bunker had to be somewhere underneath.

Maya had her gun in her hands as she moved forward, tiptoeing her way past tripwires, sidestepping a cluster of bunny rabbits playing in the field in front. Maya crept forward, doing everything she could to keep out of sight.

She saw a camera and picked up a rock, throwing it with the speed and precision of a baseball pitcher's fastball. It slammed into the side of the camera, knocking it out of alignment so that it no longer covered the door behind it. That meant that Maya could move forward again, trying the handle of the door leading to the cabin.

To her surprise, it opened, letting her move inside cautiously, weapon held, ready to use. The interior of the cabin was just about the creepiest place Maya had ever been. Stuffed and porcelain bunny rabbits sat on every available surface. Pictures of them looked down from the walls, although it was hard to make them all out in the gloomy interior of the cabin.

One picture wasn't of a rabbit. Instead, it was a photograph of the full moon, rising above a rock formation somewhere. Maya knew that she was in the right place then. This wasn't some trap for her. Her nemesis was somewhere under this cabin.

She looked around, trying to find a way into the bunker space that she knew had to be somewhere under there. Maya found it quickly, in the form of a large iron door. This one was locked, and trapped too, with a sensor that she had no doubt was connected to explosives or worse. Maya disarmed that, and set to work on the lock. In under a minute, she had it open.

The space beyond was darker than the cabin, lit by flickering strip lights that were spaced too wide apart to truly do their job. Maya followed the stairs down, moving cautiously, weapon held ahead of her.

She knew that the Moonlight Killer was in there somewhere. She could feel it, the tension rising in her as she made her way through the bunker.

She came out into a large central space that was almost dark. A single figure stood there, masked, and wearing shapeless, dark clothes. It was him. It was the Moonlight Killer.

"Freeze!" Maya yelled.

The figure didn't stand still though, but instead came rushing at her, one hand already reaching down toward a belt filled with weapons.

Maya fired and kept on firing, the sound filling the space until it seemed that there wasn't any room left for anything else. She stood over the fallen serial killer, feeling a deep sense of satisfaction at finally bringing down this monster who had kidnapped her sister.

That was when the mask fell away, revealing Megan's face beneath…

"No!" Maya cried out, crouching over her sister's body, ignoring the way alarms were starting to sound throughout the bunker…

Maya woke up to the sound of her phone ringing. Not her main phone, though, the burner phone. She was still slumped over Sheriff Lunt's desk, and there was daylight streaming into the office through one of the windows. Someone had left a cup of coffee near her head.

Maya ignored all of that and grabbed the burner phone. It was Marco, but then, no one else had the number for this phone. Leaving her own phone on the sheriff's desk, she moved away from it to avoid the risk of it picking up the external sounds.

"Marco, hey, I was just…"

Just what? Just having strange dreams about killing her own sister, or about Megan being the Moonlight Killer? Neither was something that she wanted to explain to Marco. Either one would make it clear that she wasn't handling things well here, and that she was obsessing about the case.

"Are you all right?" she asked Marco instead. "Has something happened that I need to know about?"

"No, I'm fine," Marco assured her. "I wanted to see how you're doing. Are you at a hotel?"

"I'm at the local sheriff's office," Maya said. She didn't add that she'd stayed there all night and slept with her head on Sheriff Lunt's desk. That would only worry Marco and Maya didn't want to do that when he was still recovering from a gunshot wound.

"You're there pretty early," Marco said.

Maya checked the time: 7 a.m. Early, but not nearly enough. It meant that she only had seventeen hours left in which to catch a killer.

"I wanted to make an early start," Maya said. "I only have the rest of today and I need to find a killer when I don't really have anything to go on."

"I'm sure there must be something," Marco replied. "What have you worked out about the killer so far?"

Maya tried to get her thoughts in order. "Obviously, it's not the Moonlight Killer. Even if we didn't know that going in, the business with the promise of a romantic liaison is all wrong for him."

"He's used elaborate setups before, to kidnap people and to fool us."

"Yes, but that's not what he does with his victims," Maya said. "Those… there's something simple about it, something primal. He goes out and he hunts them, then he strikes at a spot they would be going to anyway. He takes them under the full moon, in the middle of their normal lives."

"Whereas this one lured his victim to a specific spot. Is that spot significant? Is there something in his life that might connect to it?"

"Not as far as I can see," Maya said. "Although I wonder… he had a lot of one-night stands, a lot of hookups. I wonder if he met anyone there. I've been dismissing those partners as potential killers, but maybe one of them, or a boyfriend, might be behind it, and the spot might be significant."

It felt good to have slept even a little, and it felt better to be able to bounce ideas like this off Marco.

"I have a question," Marco said. "Are there any other victims?"

"No," Maya replied. "As far as I can see, it's just this one."

"That seems odd. In most of the cases so far, we've been dealing with serial killers."

"Except in the Ann Postmartin case," Maya pointed out. The first case that they'd worked on together. Was this the Moonlight Killer's way of circling back now that he'd deprived her of Marco's help? "We know that the fact that it looks like his work matters more to him than the number of victims involved."

"Possibly," Marco said. "It just seems odd. Sure, on that first case it was a single victim, but since then, there have tended to be multiple cases."

"I'm not sure how much it changes things in this one, though," Maya said. "I'm still trying to work out what this might be about. The big romantic display suggests that this might be about someone who feels cheated by Howie, but I don't have anything real to link the most likely suspect to the crime."

"You'll have to keep looking," Marco said. "You'll find an answer, Maya, I know you will. Meanwhile, I'll look into some stuff at this end to see if I can't help."

"Are you up for that?" Maya asked. "You've just been shot."

"And there is *nothing* more boring than sitting in a hospital bed doing nothing. I'd be there to back you up if I could be. As it is, I'll just have to back you up from here."

Maya appreciated that more than she could say. She just hoped that it wouldn't cause problems. The Moonlight Killer couldn't find out that Marco was still involved. It would put both him and her sister in danger.

"I have to go," Maya said. "If you find anything make sure that you send it to this number."

"I will," Marco promised.

"And Marco, I'm really glad you're ok."

Maya hung up then. She still had work to do. She still had to find a way to work out who the killer was.

Before all that, though, there was something else she needed to do. Maya went online and looked for botanists around Washington who might know about poison sumac. Maya stopped as she came across one who seemed to be engaged in bio-mapping for the area. That sounded like exactly the kind of expert she needed. It was too early to call, but she used her burner phone to set up an email address and used it to send an email, ready to follow up later.

Dear Prof. Evangelista,

My name is Agent Maya Gray, with the FBI. I am looking for details of the locations where poison sumac grows around West Virginia in connection with a case. I'm told that it's rare here, but have been unable to find exact locations. Do you know where those locations are, and if not, can you urgently point me in the direction of anyone else who might have them?

Maya added her badge number and contact details for Samit at the task force in case the professor wanted to check if she was legitimate.

She could trust Samit with this, even if she wouldn't have entirely trusted someone like Harris or Agent Swift.

Maya hoped that it would be enough. She hoped that it would help to get her closer to the location where the Moonlight Killer was holding her sister. For now though, all she could do was send the email. She had to focus on this case, had to focus on finding a way to better understand what had happened to Howie Barnet.

There was still a killer out there somewhere in Chelslake and Maya had to think of a way to catch him.

CHAPTER THIRTEEN

Marco sat in his hospital bed, wishing that he could be over in Chelslake with Maya. He suspected that she needed him. He'd been able to hear the tension in her voice, the stress that came from trying to solve a difficult case in far too short a time.

Marco shifted in his bed, getting up, ignoring the pain that came with it from his stitches. It would still be a day or two before he was allowed to leave the hospital, but did that have to stop him from helping?

He couldn't do anything physically, couldn't be there, and not just because of the gunshot wound that had left him in the hospital, only pain meds stopping it from being too bad. He was alone, aside from the nurses who looked in on him periodically, Marco suspected slightly more often than they strictly needed to.

He grabbed his clothes, got dressed, and slipped out of the hospital room. He wanted to help Maya and he knew he couldn't do it from within a place that would be too easy for the Moonlight Killer to watch.

He couldn't give the Moonlight Killer any chance to learn that Marco was trying to help Maya, and not just because of the attack that Marco had already suffered. Marco didn't care about that. He'd known that there was danger in all of this from the start. Hunting a serial killer was never going to be easy, and this was one who had managed to gain almost total control over Maya and her investigations.

No, Marco was worried because of the way the Moonlight Killer might lash out at his hostages, or at Maya directly. It already made his heart tighten in his chest to know that the Moonlight Killer had managed to isolate Maya, leaving her out there alone, with no backup. Marco was worried that all of this was designed to get Maya into a position where the Moonlight Killer could try to murder her. The thought of anything happening to Maya was almost too much to bear.

Would the Moonlight Killer target her like that, or was this case about something simpler and crueler? Was it about trying to make sure that Maya didn't have the resources that she needed to succeed? About trying to force her to fail, so that he could kill one of his captives, knowing that Maya would tear herself apart over it?

Marco couldn't allow that to happen. If he wasn't there to make sure that Maya stayed safe, then the best he could do was try to find information that might give Maya a head start in the case.

Reyes was outside Marco's room. He frowned as Marco came out of it.

"Are you meant to be up and about?"

Marco made himself shrug casually, not wanting to give Reyes a sign that he was working on anything urgent. Agent Reyes had shown several times that he wasn't good at keeping things to himself.

"I'm not a prisoner in there, Reyes, and I need to walk and stretch out. I can't just sit in bed until they release me. If it were possible, I'd be out there in Chelslake with Maya, working."

"Maybe it's just as well that you aren't," Reyes said. "You don't want to be caught up in the way things are going at the moment."

"What does that mean?" Marco asked.

"I'm just saying that you shouldn't expect that task force of yours to be around for much longer. I saw Harris and Agent Swift talking earlier. Neither of them looked happy."

That was another worry to add to the list. Marco was the only person other than Maya and the Moonlight Killer who knew about the latter's involvement in all of this, but if Agent Swift was sniffing around, that suggested that she and Harris were close to working it out. If that happened, Marco doubted that the task force would last much longer.

"Thanks for the heads up," Marco said. "Now, I'm going to get some air."

There was a small garden in the central courtyard of the hospital, hemmed in on all sides by the building's different wings. Marco walked in that garden, less interested in the air than in the chance to make a call without the risk of being overheard, either by the Moonlight Killer or by Reyes. Marco had no doubt that the latter would convey anything he overheard straight back to Harris.

There was a small bench there and Marco sat on it as he took out his phone. His stitches were aching a little, but as far as he was concerned, that was a good thing. Proof that he was alive when things could very easily have gone another way. If Maya hadn't arrived when she did, he might have bled out on the floor of his apartment.

Without her, his whole life would have been very different. She was, in her way, a force of nature. She'd come to Cleveland and solved a murder that he'd never been allowed to keep looking at. She'd pulled Marco into her orbit, and he'd followed her across half the country, chasing killers. Chasing *one* killer in particular.

Now, though, Maya needed his help to find a different one. One who seemed to have only killed a single victim, but Marco wasn't sure if he believed that. The Moonlight Killer had been sending them after serial killers, even when it initially seemed as if the cases were more straightforward than that. Marco made a call, hearing the phone ring for several seconds until Samit picked up on the other end.

"Samit, it's me," Marco said.

"Detective Spinelli!" Samit sounded relieved, as if he hadn't been expecting to hear Marco's voice so soon. "I'm glad you're ok. You *are* ok, right? Or at least as ok as you can be, after getting shot?"

"I'm fine," Marco assured him. He wasn't sure if that was completely true, but it was easier than admitting just how much his assailant had succeeded in hurting him. Marco would make the Moonlight Killer pay for that, as well as for everything else he'd done in making Marco and Maya dance to his tune. "How are things back at the office?"

Marco heard the hesitation on the other end of the line.

"What is it, Samit?"

"Agent Harris has been in. He's demanding the files related to our investigations."

This suggested that the suspicions were growing there, but Marco knew that there wasn't anything in the files that would incriminate him or Maya. They'd kept their suspicions regarding the identity of the kidnapper to themselves.

"Then you have to hand them over," Marco said. "But right now, I need something from you. Or rather, Maya does. We need to find a way to move her ahead with this investigation. Something that will give her a chance of finishing it today."

"What did you have in mind?" Samit asked.

"I need you to run a search for me for any major crimes committed in or around Chelslake. We're looking for murders or serious assaults involving strangulation. Probably of a man."

"How far back should I go?" Samit asked.

Marco tried to decide. If this was a killer who had struck before, then the cases could go back a while, potentially even years.

"Start by looking in the last two years. I get the impression that it's a quiet town, so there shouldn't be many cases."

"On it now," Samit said. There was a brief pause, in which Marco heard the sound of typing on the other end of the line. "Ok, we have fewer than ten cases involving strangulation in that time period. A couple of robberies where the victim was grabbed by the throat, some domestic battery cases…"

"Ignore those," Marco said. His instincts as a cop said that those weren't relevant here. They were serious cases in their own right, but didn't seem as though they might be connected to the murder at hand. "In fact, ignore anything where the suspect is in prison, too. We're looking for things that are potentially unsolved, cases where there wasn't much in the way of evidence."

"Got one," Samit said. "It's from around a year ago. A murder."

"A murder?"

"A young chef named Danny West was found strangled to death in the kitchen where he worked. A ligature was found around his neck."

Which gave the case obvious similarities to the one that Maya was currently looking into.

"I'm surprised the police didn't consider the possibility of a link," Marco said. "Wouldn't it have been flagged up as a potential Moonlight Killer case, the same as the death of Howie Barnet?"

"There's nothing on the case file to suggest that it was," Samit said. "Maybe because it was indoors? It looks as though the investigation mostly focused on the possibility of organized crime involvement."

Meaning that unless Marco gave Maya the file, there was no chance that anyone would make the connection between the two cases. Of course, Marco didn't know for sure that there *was* a connection. He was guessing, based on what he knew about the kind of cases the Moonlight Killer had sent them on before. A murder so long ago didn't necessarily have to have anything to do with one that had taken place only two months ago. It was possible that sending this one to Maya would only confuse things.

Yet Marco knew that he had to. His instincts said that in a place as small as Chelslake, it was asking too much of coincidence to suggest that two men could be strangled in the same way, even a year apart, and the two cases not have something to do with one another.

"Shall I forward the files to Agent Gray?" Samit asked.

"No," Marco said hurriedly. "Send them to me. I'll send them on to her. I have a method that won't be traced."

"Traced?" Samit said, sounding surprised.

"The kidnapper has insisted that she work alone on this one. We think he's watching her. We can't afford the risk of helping her too openly."

"Understood," Samit said. "I'll forward you the files now. And then, I'll run a sweep on our systems to make sure that no one is listening in."

Marco was grateful for that. Maybe if they could close the Moonlight Killer out, they would be free to act without his interference. Until then, Marco just hoped that the new case file would help to point Maya in the right direction.

CHAPTER FOURTEEN

Maya started as her burner phone alerted her to the fact that she had a message. She had only called Marco a little while ago and now there was a message for her? Maya found herself hoping that it was from him, and not just because she missed having him there with her.

If it wasn't him, then it would be either the Moonlight Killer or her bosses, having found out that she was using the burner phone to try to communicate secretly on the case. Neither would be good.

Maya breathed a sigh of relief as she saw that the message was indeed from Marco. It was short and to the point, and more than that, it suggested that Marco had found something.

Look into Danny West, killed a year ago by strangulation.

A man strangled a year ago? That seemed a long time ago for a killer who was active without any obvious other kills on file, but Maya guessed that there must have been plenty about the murder to excite Marco when he saw it, or he wouldn't be forwarding it to her now.

A part of Maya wanted to call Marco to find out, but she could guess how dangerous that might prove. Maya had already been away from her main phone for several minutes, and if she pushed it much longer, there was a chance that the Moonlight Killer was going to become suspicious. No, she needed to head back there and do this herself.

Maya went back to the desk, being careful to silence the burner phone so that any sound from it wouldn't be picked up by the bug in her main one. She drank the coffee that someone had left for her gratefully, then went looking for Sheriff Lunt. She found him in the reception area of the sheriff's station, looking considerably brighter and happier than she currently felt. But then, he hadn't been the one sleeping at his desk last night.

"How are you doing this morning, Agent Gray?" he asked. "Looks like you put in the hours last night."

Not as many as Maya had been hoping for. She had thought that she could work right through until morning, but her own body had betrayed her, demanding sleep.

"I need to ask you about a case," Maya said. "One I hope you might remember."

"You didn't just look it up in the system?" the sheriff said.

Maya hadn't, but she needed to lie about it. If the Moonlight Killer was listening in, then she needed to make it seem as if she'd come up with this through her own research, rather than being given it by Marco. It made the whole conversation potentially tricker.

"I looked at your system, looking for other cases in which someone had been strangled. A name came up, from about a year ago. Danny West. Now, I'd appreciate anything you can remember about the case. I want to get your impressions."

"West… West…" The sheriff stood there for a moment or two, staring into space as he thought. "Yes, I remember. Danny West, 26. He was the chef down at Hepple's restaurant. One of the servers came into the kitchen and found that he'd been strangled from behind, a ligature wrapped around his neck. But what do you think it has to do with this case? It was in the middle of the day, not under the full moon."

"That would only be relevant if the Howie Barnet case were down to the Moonlight Killer, and it's not."

Maya hadn't been that interested in the case until the sheriff mentioned the ligature, or the way the chef had just been found, obviously ambushed. Now, though, she was starting to think that there was a possibility that the cases might be linked, exactly as Marco had said.

"The case is still unsolved, right?" Maya said. She doubted that Marco would have sent her a case where the killer had already been caught.

"We could never find a suspect," the sheriff said. "There were rumors about West owing the wrong people money, but other than that? No real enemies, no physical evidence. No security footage that told us anything useful. You really think that this is linked?"

"You said it when I got here, Sheriff, Chelslake is a quiet town. I know it's a year ago, but really, what are the odds of two murders of young men using the same method in one small town?"

Maya saw the sheriff's eyes widen as the truth of it started to sink in. "Not that good. What now?"

"Now, I'm going to go to Hepple's restaurant, see if I can find anything else," Maya said. "Maybe the staff there will remember something that will help to open up both of these cases."

*

Hepple's bar and restaurant looked to Maya as if it was doing pretty well, for a place whose chef had been murdered a year ago. It sat in the middle of a small row of other places obviously designed to cater to the tourists who visited the town. It was open and already busy with what looked like a regular breakfast crowd.

The interior was light and airy, with walls painted pale gray and small, circular tables dotted around the floor. A bar sat at one end, but for the moment, the customers there all seemed to be drinking coffee. There were pictures around the walls that were a mixture of photographs of boats out on the lake and watercolors presumably by local artists, but Maya didn't have any time to stand and appreciate them; she only had today in which to solve the murder she'd been sent here for, and she didn't even know if this place was related yet.

The manager, a blonde-haired young woman, a little shorter than Maya with angular features and deep blue eyes, met Maya as she stepped into the place.

"Are you here for breakfast, ma'am? Sit anywhere you like."

"Thanks, but I'm not here for the food," Maya said, showing her badge. "You're the manager?"

She nodded. "I'm Imogen Hepple, yes.

I need to speak to you. It's about Danny West."

Maya saw the shock on the young woman's face.

"I… wasn't expecting to hear anything else about that," she said. "The sheriff's department didn't think that there were any leads."

"I look at cold cases," Maya said, "and I think that this one may be linked to another case I'm working on."

The manager nodded, as if that all made sense to her, but there was a blank element to her expression that suggested that she was still slightly in shock from Maya announcing the reason she was there.

"Were you here when Danny was found?" Maya asked.

Imogen nodded. "It was me… I was the one who found him."

Maya could only imagine how much of an impact that moment would have had on her. Maya had been hardened by years in the military and the FBI, but finding a body still had an effect on her. For someone who had found a friend or a colleague dead, it was probably still having an effect.

"Do you feel like you're able to talk me through it all?" Maya asked. "Could you maybe show me the spot where it happened?"

Imogen nodded after a moment or two.

"Ok, come on back to the kitchen. We're in the middle of breakfast and prep for later, so it will be a little busy, but we should be able to show you the spot."

She led the way through the restaurant, so that Maya had to weave her way through the diners to get to the kitchen. The interior was bright and modern, with pristine stainless steel surfaces everywhere. There were a couple of chefs there working together, a man and a woman, while a kitchen assistant was off to one side, chopping vegetables. They were moving smoothly around one another, but Maya found that she had to tread carefully to avoid bumping into them.

"Is it always crowded in here?" Maya asked. "Was it like this a year ago?"

If so, she had a hard time imagining how someone could have gotten in there to kill Danny West.

"It was in one of our quiet periods, and Danny mostly worked alone," Imogen said. "I would help with some of the prep in the morning, and we had a kitchen assistant who came in for the evening, but in between, it was just Danny."

Meaning that the killer had known when he had the time to make the kill. He'd been watching his target.

"Do you know if Danny had any enemies?" Maya asked.

"The cops asked me that," Imogen said. "All I could think of was… well, Danny had debts. He liked to gamble. He asked me for money a couple of times, but I couldn't help him. I didn't think it was a good idea. I wish I had."

"You think that someone might have killed him over his debts?" Maya said.

"I don't know. I don't even know who he left the restaurant to go see," Imogen said.

Maya frowned at that. "Left the restaurant?"

“I caught a glimpse of him outside the restaurant about five minutes before I found him,” Imogen said. “I told the police this, but I’m not sure if they did anything with it. I thought maybe he’d gone out to talk to someone he owed money to.”

Maya considered that when they’d realized that they weren’t going to get their money, they’d followed him back into the restaurant and strangled him, through an entrance that wasn’t covered by security cameras.

It was a possible hypothesis, but Maya couldn’t see the evidence for it beyond Danny West’s debts. She would need to chase down those debts, but the more she looked at this, the closer the method of the murder and the appearance of the two victims seemed. Moment by moment, it seemed more likely to her that that this case was connected to the Howie Barnet one.

Which meant that Maya had to make a decision. She only had the rest of today to devote to this case. Did she throw her efforts into the Howie Barnet case and hope that she found something, or did she look at this new case on the basis of a connection that might or might not be there?

If there *was* a connection, this new case might give her a way in. She had to at least try looking at it.

CHAPTER FIFTEEN

Now that Maya had seen the site of the murder, she wanted to look deeper into it. She wanted to get the details to see if there was anything there that might make sense when compared to the details of the Howie Barnet case. Maybe there was something that hadn't seemed like anything important at the time, but which might match up with something from the more recent case to let her move forward.

Maya went back to her car and grabbed her laptop, pulling up the file from the Danny West case alongside the one from the Howie Barnet one. She started to read through them, trying to work out just how far Sheriff Lunt had gotten with the case before he'd concluded that there wasn't any more progress to be made.

There was a picture of the victim at the top and, for a moment, Maya thought that she must have opened the wrong file by mistake. But no, it really was a picture of Danny West, dark-haired and handsome, slightly youthful looking for his age. He looked a lot like Howie Barnet. A lot.

Was that significant? It seemed like another connection between the cases, one that made it seem almost certain now that the two had to be linked. It seemed like an impossible coincidence that two men who looked so similar could have been killed by entirely separate killers.

If the killings were linked, was it significant that there was a potential existing motive for someone to want to kill Danny West? Given how similar he looked to Howie Barnet, was it possible that someone had mistakenly thought that he *was Danny*?

Was that really a possibility? Was it possible that the man who had killed Danny West had seen Howie Barnet and thought that he'd somehow made a mistake, that he'd missed his target? Had he thought that all the press coverage there surely would have been around Danny West's death had been fake?

It was a longshot, but right then, it was all that Maya had. So was her best move right then to try to work out who Danny West had owed money to? There were plenty of references in the file to how broke

Danny was, how bad his gambling had become. He'd been an addict, unable to stop himself from gambling in spite of going to meetings and trying to change his behavior. He sounded like the kind of guy who'd always been in debt to someone, whether it was friends, family, or bookies.

The question was who his bookie had been at the time of his death. There wasn't a note about that in the file, which might mean that nobody knew; but maybe that just meant that it was someone that no one was prepared to talk about, certainly not complain about to the police. Maybe the lack of a name was itself an indication of just how dangerous this person was.

The question was how to find out about someone like that after all this time. Maya didn't know the local area's criminal underworld, and it seemed obvious that Sheriff Lunt couldn't get people in it to talk, or he would already have found answers. Maya guessed that most people would be scared to say anything, or wouldn't know anything.

She needed to find someone who was prepared to talk to her, someone who knew Danny West well enough that they might know who his bookie had been. Preferably someone who might know if he had any other enemies, or who would have been in a position to kill him.

Maya needed to talk to Danny West's family.

Maya found an address for Danny West's parents in the file and drove over to their house. The family home was on a quiet road a little outside the main town. It was a broad, low building, seemingly all built on one level, with a large garage at one side. Maya spotted a couple of cars there as she pulled up, suggesting that someone was probably home.

Maya rang the doorbell and waited. A woman in her fifties answered. She was short and dark-haired, slender and dark-eyed, wearing a simple dark outfit.

"Yes?"

Maya held up her badge. "I'm Agent Gray, with the FBI. I need to talk with the family of Danny West."

"I'm Veronica West, Daniel's mother," the woman said. "The FBI is investigating my son's death now?"

Maya nodded. "It appears that there may be a connection to another case, but to establish that, I need-"

"Veronica, who is it?" It was a man's voice, big and booming.

"It's the FBI, Clifford." Veronica West stepped aside to let Maya pass. "You'd better come in."

She showed Maya into the house. To Maya, the whole place looked expensively appointed, professionally decorated in neutral shades, with ornaments here and there that were clearly antiques.

Maya followed Veronica into a lounge that was so pristine and elegant it was hard to imagine anyone actually living there. It seemed more like the kind of place someone might receive a visiting head of state if they were trying to be informal about it. Every piece of furniture looked antique, while there were pictures around the walls of the Wests with a variety of important looking figures. Maya even recognized some of them.

She *couldn't* spot any pictures of Danny West, which caught her a little by surprise.

There was a man there waiting for her, in his fifties like Veronica, square-jawed and dark-haired, with a build that suggested he'd been athletic in his youth and maybe even still worked out, but not quite enough to offset large dinners. He was wearing dark slacks and a light shirt that he'd rolled up to the elbows. He regarded Maya with a cautious expression before gesturing to one of the chairs set around the room.

"You're here to talk about our son, Agent…"

"Gray, Mr. West." Maya took the offered seat, while Clifford and Veronica West sat together on an elegantly minimalist couch.

"You're looking into his death?" Steel gray eyes bored into hers, obviously trying to find out the truth of the situation.

"His death has shown some similarities to another case I'm working on," Maya explained, not wanting to give away too many details but also wanting to be as honest as she could about all of this. "My belief is that the two cases may be connected, and that by looking at them together, I might be able to make some progress."

"Does it occur to you that maybe the past is better left in the past?"

Maya had heard similar sentiments from those around cold cases before, although rarely put quite so bluntly. Often, she came into cases just as the wounds of the past were starting to heal, so that families viewed her presence not as an opportunity for closure, but as an intrusion into their affairs, causing them unnecessary pain.

"Sometimes, we need to reopen the wounds of the past to close them properly," Maya said. "Don't you want to see the man who did this to your son behind bars, Mr. West?"

She saw Clifford West bristle slightly at that, leaning forward slightly in his seat. "If I thought there was a chance of him actually seeing the inside of a jail, of course I'd want it. As it is, all your presence here is likely to do is cause trouble for all of us."

"What kind of trouble?" Maya asked, hoping to get to an answer that way.

Clifford West shook his head, though. "The kind that will still be here for us once the FBI is gone from Chelslake. The kind that would make important people wonder if it was good to be associated with us."

Maya found herself glancing at the photographs on the walls.

"Can you at least tell me about your son, Mr. West?" Maya asked.

"Daniel was… well, troubled," Clifford said. "We did our best to raise him right, gave him every advantage. The plan was that he would be a lawyer like his mother, or a political consultant like me."

Maya found herself wondering if that had been Clifford's plan or Danny's.

"So what happened?" Maya asked.

"Danny always wanted to go his own way," Veronica West said. "He wanted to find his own path through the world."

"And we supported him for most of it," Clifford West put in. "When he wanted to take a year out to go find himself. When he decided that he wanted to be a cook, rather than any of the other things he could have been."

"So, what happened?" Maya asked. There had to be a reason that there were no photographs of Danny West on the walls.

"If you know anything about our son at all, then you *know* what happened," Clifford West shot back. "The gambling."

Maya had heard about Danny's gambling, but it seemed that no one was willing to go into the specifics of it all.

"What can you tell me about his gambling?" Maya asked.

"Just that it ruined our relationship with our son," Clifford West said. "He gambled on anything he could find: horses, fights, cards. And he lost. He lost continuously. He lost more than he could afford. Enough that he started to borrow money from us, then steal. For a while, we let him stay in our garage, but eventually, we had to cut him off."

Maya could see the pain in Veronica West's face as her husband said it. "Maybe if we'd let him stay, things wouldn't have turned out the way they did."

Her husband's hand closed over hers. "We've been through this, Veronica. There was nothing we could do to help until he was ready to help himself. We had to show him tough love."

"How tough?" Maya asked.

"We cut him off," Clifford said. "No money, no place to stay, no chance to steal from us to pay his debts."

"So he *did* have debts?" Maya said, trying to push the conversation back in the direction she needed.

She saw Clifford nod.

"Do you know who he owed money to?" Maya asked.

Now, Clifford shook his head. "Like I said before, we still have to live here after the FBI has gone."

"But-"

"No. I think you should leave, now, Agent Gray."

"Mr. West-"

"No. Please leave." Mr. West stood up now, gesturing towards the door.

"I'll show her out, Clifford," Veronica West said. "Don't get yourself so worked up. You know what the doctor said about your blood pressure."

She led Maya toward the door and Maya didn't really have an option except to follow. She reached the door and saw Mrs. West hesitate, looking worried, even frightened.

She leaned closer to Maya, lowering her voice to a whisper. "Gus Scarrat. My son owed money to a man named Gus Scarrat. He told me that he owed him; he asked for money. He told us he was scared. That's all I can say."

Maya found herself wondering how frightening this man was that even Danny West's parents barely dared to speak about him. Clearly, he was someone dangerous. Dangerous enough that, under other circumstances, Maya might have thought twice about going to see him.

Instead, she went back to her car and put in a call to Sheriff Lunt.

"Agent Gray, what can I do for you?"

"What can you tell me about Gus Scarrat?" Maya asked.

"Where did you hear that name?"

"Danny West owed him money. Now, tell me about him."

There was a moment of hesitation on the other end of the line.

"This is a dangerous man to start asking after, Agent Gray. He's nominally a bar owner, of *Gus's* bar, but there's a gambling club underneath and…"

"And he's the local gangster?" Maya guessed. She'd met men like that before.

"Don't underestimate him," Sheriff Lunt said. "He doesn't care who he hurts. Even my deputies don't go into his businesses uninvited. It's too dangerous."

Maya could hear the fear there, and she guessed that the sheriff wouldn't sound that frightened without good reason. Worse, she was alone here. If she'd had Marco backing her up, this would have been an easy choice, but alone… she might walk into Gus Scarrat's place and never walk out.

Maya knew that she didn't have a choice, though. Her sister was in danger. She had to go to the bar. She had to go talk to Gus Scarrat, because if she didn't make some progress on this case, her sister was going to die.

CHAPTER SIXTEEN

It wasn't hard for Maya to find the bar that Gus Scarrat conducted his business out of. It was on one of the smaller back streets of the town, but there were people moving in and out of it quite openly as Maya approached. Even though it was still just the morning, it was busy. Apparently, the gambling business was open at all times.

Maya paused outside, considering her next moves. The bar was cleaner than she'd expected it to be, not grimy or run down, but perhaps that just said how good business was for the town's criminals. She could try to enter the place quietly to look around, but in the absence of a warrant, that wasn't an option that would get her very far. It was also the option that exposed her to the most danger.

She could walk in the front with her badge out, declaring that she was FBI from the start. That ran into the same problem of lack of a warrant. She probably wouldn't even get to speak to Gus Scarrat. It might be her safest option, but it wouldn't let Maya get any further with the case.

That left one option: walking in there as a potential customer, getting to speak to Scarrat, and only then declaring who she was. It was still potentially dangerous. If this man was as big of a threat as the sheriff seemed to think, then there was a risk that he would try to kill Maya just for doing something like that.

Yet it also seemed like her best chance of getting to talk to him face to face, and if he was really as dangerous as the sheriff said, then that was all the more reason to consider him a possible suspect in the murder. Maya couldn't waste any more time standing out here thinking about it; she had to act, now.

Making sure that she could get to her gun easily, Maya walked into the bar. The interior was lined with booths, the leather of the seats almost worn out with age. There were TVs around the walls, all showing different sporting events. A few people stared up at them in hope or with something more blank, the dead look of someone chasing too many losses. There was a bar at one end, and the bartender nodded to Maya as she approached.

"What can I get you to drink?"

Maya had already spotted a door off to the side, though, one that a man stepped through as she watched, heading down a set of stairs towards what was presumably a basement level.

"I'm not here to drink," Maya said, and headed for the door.

"Hey, you don't want to go down there," the bartender said, starting towards her.

Maya fixed him in place with a look that made it clear it would not be a good idea for him to touch her. He seemed to get the message, backing off with his hands raised.

"Don't say I didn't warn you."

Maya headed for the stairs leading down into the basement. There, she wasn't at all surprised to find card and roulette tables set up, people clustered around them gambling even though it was still early in the day.

Several of them looked up as Maya entered the room. Maya could sense the instant hostility from some of them, glares shooting her way, along with suspicious stares. It was obvious that at least some of the people there knew exactly who Maya was. Certainly a couple of bigger men lounging at the side seemed to have worked out that she was law enforcement, because they moved to intercept her. One had a shaved head and jowly features, while the other was dark-haired and muscled like a bodybuilder.

"You a cop?" the one with the shaven head asked.

"Nothing so simple," Maya replied. She flashed her badge. "FBI."

"We don't want you in here," the bodybuilder said, and he reached out to grab Maya's arm.

Maya twisted out of his grip and stepped in behind his foot to trip him, slamming her hand up under his jaw as she did it to shove him back. He tumbled to the floor and instantly, Maya grabbed his arm, twisting it to the very edge of breaking.

"What you don't want is the kind of trouble that will come from messing with an FBI agent in the middle of a murder investigation," Maya said. "I am *not* the local sheriff. I won't back off because it's more convenient. And if you touch me again, I'll haul you down to the local jail, charge you with obstruction, and come back with a warrant to tear this place apart."

Maya let go and stepped back, giving herself as much room as she could to react if the thug decided that he wanted to try grabbing her again. Some of the other people around the room were staring at her, but others were already focusing on gambling again. Maybe pointedly so, like they didn't want to get involved in anything that wasn't to do with them.

That worried Maya in its own way because it reminded her what kind of place this was. It was somewhere that, if she went missing, no one would admit to having seen her there. There certainly wouldn't be any security footage, because if a place like this had cameras at all, the footage of anything incriminating would always conveniently go missing before the cops got there.

There was another door at the far side of the room, this one looking like it led to an office. Maya stepped over to it and opened the door, keeping one eye on the two thugs outside as she stepped into the space beyond.

It *was* an office, with a man seated behind a large desk off to one side, away from the door, as if not wanting to be in the line of fire if someone burst in shooting. He was a large man in his forties, balding, and with a dark beard. He was wearing a dark suit that seemed barely big enough to contain his muscles, while the dark brown of his eyes were filled with hostility as they fixed on Maya. This was obviously Gus Scarrat.

"Who are you and what are you doing in my office?" he demanded. He looked at her for another second or two. "You're not a local cop, so what are you? FBI?"

Maya took out her badge. "Agent Maya Gray. FBI. I'm here to talk to you about Danny West, Mr. Scarrat."

"And what makes you think I want to talk to you about him?" Scarrat stood then, obviously trying to use his size to intimidate Maya.

"Because it would be bad for business if you don't," Maya said. "You've been dealing with the local sheriff so far, Mr. Scarrat, but what do you think will happen if I put in a call to one of the FBI's organized crime teams and have them put their full attention on you?"

"They would find nothing. I am a respectable businessman."

He managed to say that with a straight face, in spite of the gambling ring Maya had just walked through on the way in.

"I don't have time to play games, Mr. Scarrat," Maya said. "Tell me about Danny West, or I'll make it my business to tear apart *your* business."

Maya saw the bookie's features harden into a mask of anger. "Danny West was scum who didn't pay his debts. He lost when he gambled and then he went and died before I could collect the money I was owed."

"Or did he die *because* he couldn't pay you?" Maya countered. That was the big question, the suspicion that hung over all of this. "Did you kill him to make an example of him, so that other people would pay up quicker?"

Scarrat settled back into his seat, making a show of how relaxed he was. It was probably designed to make him seem more honest, but Maya didn't believe it for an instant.

"Are you recording any of this, Agent Gray?"

Maya shook her head. "I just want answers."

"Then I'll say this much openly, if I had killed Danny West, do you think I would have done it in such a stupid way? Strangled at work and left? What kind of example would that set?"

"So you're saying that because he wasn't killed publicly or beaten to death or something, it couldn't have been down to you?" Maya said.

"Or disappeared," Scarrat added. His hand reached down into a desk drawer, and Maya realized almost too late that he was pulling a weapon. She tried to clear her own gun, but the big man was faster.

Maya could only stand there, her heart hammering in her chest as she stood at gunpoint.

"If I wanted," Scarrat said, "I could shoot you and no one would ever know it happened. You would simply disappear, like you were never here."

Maya wondered then just how much of a mistake she'd made by coming there. Was she going to make it out of there, and if she didn't, what did that mean for her sister and the other women the Moonlight Killer had as his hostages?

"The sheriff knows I was coming here," Maya said, "and the moment he passes that information along to the FBI, your life is over."

"Do you really think he'll do anything except what I tell him?" Scarrat demanded.

"What about Howie Barnet?" If she was already in trouble, Maya was at least going to keep asking questions. "Did you kill him?"

"Barnet? The young man who died a couple of months back?" Scarrat laughed then. "Is that what this is really about? That waste of breath Danny West isn't worth a real investigation, but someone else dies, and now the FBI are involved? No, I didn't have anything to do with his death. Again, do you think I would be that elaborate? Besides, he didn't owe me money."

Maya wondered if that were true, but Scarrat had a point: he wouldn't lure someone to an island through an elaborate catfishing scheme. He would just have his men pick Barnet up and kill him quietly, or shoot him in the street.

"I was working on the theory that maybe you or your men thought that Howie Barnet was somehow Danny West, having survived what you did to him."

"Now you're insulting my intelligence, Agent Gray," Scarrat said. "This is my town. I know who the people are here. I'm not going to be fooled because two people look vaguely similar. And if I want someone dead, do you really think I wouldn't be thorough about it? Do you think I would leave any room for doubt?"

Maya had to admit that he had a point there. Of course, it didn't make the fact that he was currently pointing a gun her way any easier to deal with. If his aim wavered even for a moment, she could draw her Glock, but for now, he had her dead to rights. All he had to do was pull the trigger.

"The question is what I do with you," Scarrat said.

"That comes down to how much trouble you want," Maya replied. This was not a moment to show even a hint of weakness. "Yes, you could shoot me, but are you *really* sure that you can keep the full weight of the FBI from landing at your door if you do that?"

"And if I don't, my business gets picked apart anyway," Scarrat said.

"I got what I wanted here," Maya replied. "I'm not interested in your business. I'm interested in catching a murderer."

It was her best shot at getting out of here alive. Even so, as the seconds stretched out, Maya wondered in growing terror if it would be enough.

The flood of relief that swept through her as Scarrat put down the gun was almost too much to bear.

"All right," he said. "Get out. But if I see you near my business again…"

He didn't finish the threat. He didn't need to.

Maya hurried out of the room, still half expecting him to shoot her in the back as she left. She left the bar as quickly as she could, leaning against a wall outside and breathing hard.

Maya wasn't sure how much of what Gus Scarrat had said to her was true, but parts of it had seemed far too credible. He had no obvious reason to want to hurt Howie Barnet, and he was right; this kind of murder wasn't what a gangster like him would do to make an example of someone.

It was the kind of thing that Maya should have worked out before coming here, but the time pressure was getting to her, forcing her into decisions that she wouldn't have made otherwise.

It was a dead end, and one that had almost cost Maya her life.

CHAPTER SEVENTEEN

Benjamin Malt wasn't entirely sure what he was doing out here, in a field containing little other than a solar panel array, the sunlight reflecting off it until it was bright enough to hurt his eyes.

It had all seemed like such a good idea last night. He would meet up with a hot young woman, one who was clearly pretty adventurous if her messages to him had been anything to go by, and probably have… well, at the very least, a story that he could tell the guys. Maybe more than that, depending on how things went.

Maybe he should just have met up with her last night, but Benjamin wasn't quite intrepid enough to go meeting up with strange women outdoors in the middle of the night. There was always too much of a risk that it was a scam, or just something designed to make him look stupid.

The choice of spot today didn't exactly fill Benjamin with confidence. A field? Sure, they could have a picnic or something. Hell, he'd *brought* a picnic, with a few sandwiches, a couple of bottles of beer, just something to set the mood. But a field with one of the big solar arrays that lay scattered around the town to provide it with some of its power?

Maybe the point was that they would be harder to spot there; maybe the idea was to give them both at least the illusion of privacy. Besides, he'd promised Izzie online that she was the one who got to pick the spot. If this was what she was into, then he would find a way to work with that.

"Izzie?" Benjamin called out. "I'm here!"

She had to be here somewhere, and it wouldn't exactly be easy to spot her among the solar panels that made up the array. Maybe she was heading towards him now, or sneaking up on him. Maybe that was a part of the game that she wanted to play here.

If it had been a different girl, Benjamin might have just headed home. He generally liked things a lot more straightforward than this. But some of those pictures she'd sent over to him… she'd been so hot, and her messages had made it clear that she was more than interested in him. She seemed to know exactly what she wanted, and it lined up with everything *he* wanted from today, too.

So Benjamin played along for now. He wandered through the solar panels, trying not to look around too carefully, letting her think that she could sneak up on him. Maybe he could catch her out as she did so, and see where things led from there…

Benjamin stood there thinking about the possibilities of that. He looked into one of the solar panels, using its surface as a mirror, adjusting his hair slightly to make sure that it was perfect.

He saw a flicker of movement in the reflection and started to smile as he began to turn.

"Izzie, is that-"

He didn't finish the sentence, because that was the moment that a cord dropped around his throat, drawing tight.

CHAPTER EIGHTEEN

Maya drove well away from the bar as she tried to work out what to do next. She could still feel the adrenaline flooding her body from having been held at gunpoint, making her grip the wheel tight enough that her knuckles went white with it.

A part of her wanted to charge back into Gus Scarrat's place and arrest him just for threatening her, going in there with her weapon already drawn, ready to take down any of his thugs who got in her way. Maya knew that was just her natural reaction to being made to feel afraid, though.

In reality, she didn't have enough evidence to bring him in for anything, and charging in there would just be her way of showing that she wasn't afraid, picking a fight for the sake of it. It was a course of action that would probably lead to Maya shooting one or more of his bodyguards, if not Scarrat himself, and then where would she be? Left facing an inquiry into her use of lethal force when she should be finding a killer and trying to get her sister back.

That was a part of why she needed to be away from the bar: not because she was scared of Gus Scarrat, but because Maya was scared of what she might do if she stayed there.

He probably wasn't the killer she was looking for in any case. Maya needed to find a new angle on all of this. She just wasn't sure where to start. She got out her burner phone, ready to call Marco, then saw that there was an email waiting for her there.

That caught Maya a little by surprise until she remembered the email that she'd sent to the biologist who was an expert on rare poisonous plant species. Was it possible that there was an answer waiting for Maya already?

Maya opened the email eagerly, caught between hope and apprehension. She hoped that this would be the answer she had been looking for, the one that would allow her to locate her sister. She feared that this email might not be from the expert she'd contacted at all, but might instead be from the Moonlight Killer, telling her that he knew what she'd done and sending pictures of his retaliation against her sister.

Maya's relief was almost overwhelming as she opened the email and found that it was indeed from Professor Evangelista, the expert she'd contacted. That feeling was quickly followed by a hungry need to know exactly what the professor had found out. If the professor had answers for her, Maya wanted them.

Dear Agent Gray,

I can confirm that the plant poison sumac does indeed exist in limited numbers in West Virginia, and that the research of some of my colleagues has included cataloging them. I have included a list of the locations below. While this list is unlikely to be exhaustive, I hope that you find it of use.

Prof. Evangelista.

There was a list of locations below, exactly as the professor had promised. It wasn't a long list, maybe twenty or thirty locations, each highly specific and limited to just a few plants.

In other words, it was exactly the kind of thing that might allow Maya to find the location where her sister and the others were being held.

Maya got out her computer, calling up her map of locations for the saw-whet owl. Then she realized that there was a chance that the Moonlight Killer was able to look in on her computer, the way he did with her phone. She couldn't input the locations of the poison sumac on the map on her screen because that would make it too obvious to him that she was closing in on him.

Maya could have left it until tomorrow, but she couldn't bring herself to do it. She needed to give herself the opportunity to get to her sister if this case didn't work out. She needed a physical map and she had no time to waste.

Maya drove until she found a local library. She grabbed her laptop but left her main phone in the car, not wanting to risk the Moonlight Killer overhearing anything that she was going to say next. Maya ran in with her laptop under her arm.

A librarian stood behind a reception desk. She was a middle-aged woman with dark hair and glasses, wearing a cardigan over a cream colored blouse and a checked skirt.

"I need a map of West Virginia," Maya said. "Urgently."

"Online maps are very-"

"Not for this," Maya said. She was in too much of a hurry to explain everything.

"Well, there are some maps towards the back over there, but-"

Maya was already heading for them, running, not wanting to waste a single moment. She reached the maps and sorted through them until she found one of West Virginia at a scale that she could work with. It needed to show the whole state, but at a close enough scale that she could pin down specific locations.

Maya took out her laptop, pulling up the image of the saw-whet owl's habitats. Taking out a pen, Maya started to circle those locations on the map. She was working quickly, but she wanted to be accurate. She didn't want to risk leaving out any location that might be the spot where the Moonlight Killer was holding the women captive.

"What do you think you're doing?" the librarian demanded. "You can't just draw on our maps!"

Maya took out her badge, holding it out as if to ward off the librarian's advance.

"FBI. This is to do with a case and lives could be at stake. We'll replace the map, but for now, I need this one."

Maya had commandeered vehicles before, but she'd never commandeered a map. This, though, could prove to be more important than anything else she'd done. This could be the moment that saved her sister's life, but only if she did this right.

Maya shut down her computer then, not wanting there to be any chance of the Moonlight Killer looking on for the next part. Maya started to draw in the spots from the list of locations where poison sumac grew, in much smaller circles than for the owl.

Each time she put one in place and it didn't intersect with one of the shapes she'd already drawn for the owl's territory, Maya cursed silently to herself. Yet she realized that it was actually a good thing. She didn't want a dozen results.

Finally, one crossed over with an owl's territory. Maya's heart was in her mouth as she drew it, but she didn't stop. She knew that there could be others. She had to work her way through the whole list.

She did, and then stared at the map in a mixture of joy and disbelief. There was only one area that contained both poison sumac and the saw-whet owl. One place in the whole of West Virginia.

Maya looked up at the librarian. "I need to borrow a computer, right now."

"But you have your laptop," the librarian said with a frown.

"And I can't *trust* that for this. It's too important."

Maya could hear the librarian grumbling as she led Maya to the computer behind the reception desk. Maya quickly accessed the internet, pulling up a map view of West Virginia and then focusing on the small area that she'd identified. She zoomed in so that the area filled the screen.

The map didn't show anything there, but Maya was convinced that she had found the right area. She switched over to a satellite view, hoping that it would show her more. The moment she did, Maya knew that she'd found the right spot.

There was a cabin there, set in a clearing. That was it, it had to be. Maya had found the place where the Moonlight Killer was holding his victims.

"Got you," Maya whispered.

Her first instinct was to call Marco, call Harris, call every kind of backup that she could find. Maya quickly squashed that instinct. She didn't want to risk Harris bungling another raid, charging in with so many agents that the Moonlight Killer heard them coming from miles away. If this really was someone with a special forces background, then he would be ready for the possibility of the FBI finding him.

Maya couldn't allow Harris and the others to ruin this. That meant that, for the moment at least, she couldn't even risk telling Marco what was going on, because he would insist on her having backup. No, Maya had to do this part alone.

Maya hurried out of the library, leaving the librarian glaring after her. She drove down to the lake, because to anyone tracking her phone, that would look convincingly like she was merely continuing her investigation. She got out of her car, taking her phone with her as she considered her options.

She had a chance, right now, to hunt the Moonlight Killer, free all his hostages, and end this. He would think that she was still looking into things here, and to keep up that pretense, Maya couldn't afford to take her phone with her. She had to destroy it, but it had to happen in a way that might conceivably look like an accident from the outside. Maya still didn't know if the Moonlight Killer had anyone watching her.

Maya got in one of the tourist boats to the island, holding her phone as she did so. Her best chance here was to drop the phone in the water as she went out to the island. To anyone watching her, that would look like an accident, at least for long enough. Maya just needed an hour or two; enough time to get to the Moonlight Killer's location, free her sister, and take him down.

Maya was just getting ready to drop the phone when it rang. Maya was tempted to drop it anyway, but then she saw the sheriff's name. She answered.

"What is it, Sheriff?"

"Agent Gray, you need to come quick. There's been another murder. Another man strangled."

Maya cursed to herself. A part of her wanted to ignore that, wanted to just go rescue her sister. She knew she couldn't, though. She could bring herself to abandon a cold case, but if there was still an active killer out there murdering people, Maya had to help to stop him before he killed anyone else. The Moonlight Killer would have to wait.

"Give me the location. I'll be right there."

CHAPTER NINETEEN

It was easy for Maya to spot the crime scene as she drove up, because it was the only real sign of human activity to be seen in any direction. There was a forensics tent set up in the middle of a field there, in what appeared to be the midst of a solar array. There were several of the sheriff's deputies standing around to secure the scene, but Maya got the feeling that they were mostly standing there because they didn't know what else to do.

Maya could see the relief on a couple of the deputies' faces as she drove up and jumped out of her car. Obviously they were happy that the FBI was there to make sense of things, but Maya wished that someone were there to help *her* make sense of it.

Not for the first time, she found herself wishing that Marco were there. Although, with what she'd just worked out in the library, Maya guessed that his presence would only have complicated things when it came to going after the Moonlight Killer. He would want Maya to have backup, and right then, Maya didn't want backup. She wanted to take the Moonlight Killer down alone.

After she'd solved this case. For now, there was still a killer out there, murdering people in Chelslake. Maya had to find him. More than that, she still had to find him by the Moonlight Killer's almost impossible deadline, because now that she wasn't going to save her sister directly, Maya still had to worry about what the Moonlight Killer might do if she didn't solve this in time.

Maya hurried to the tent that the forensics people had put in place around the body, seeing several of the coroner's people there. She was quite impressed by the efficiency of it all and by the resources that the sheriff's department was prepared to throw at something like this.

Sheriff Lunt was at the entrance to the tent, his expression grave. "Where have you been, Agent Gray?"

"You know where," Maya said. "I went to talk to Gus Scarrat."

Sheriff Lunt looked worried by that. "I told you how dangerous that might be."

"I almost found that out the hard way," Maya said. "He pulled a gun on me."

"Do you have any evidence of that?" The sheriff sounded both hopeful and worried, as if he saw his chance to finally get rid of his town's biggest problem, but also knew that it would be him who had to go in to make the actual arrest if it came to that.

Maya shook her head. "It's not important. I'm here to focus on the murders, and I don't think that Scarrat had anything to do with them. Howie Barnet didn't have any connection to him, and the style of the killing doesn't fit the idea of him punishing someone for failing to pay their debts."

The sheriff nodded, still looking a little troubled. Obviously, he was thinking about just how much trouble Maya was going to leave in her wake here. Maya could understand his concern, but right then she had her own priorities. She would do whatever it took to solve this murder and buy the time she needed to get to her sister.

"What do we have here?" Maya asked the sheriff.

"The deceased is Benjamin Malt, lived on 2nd Street back in town," the sheriff said. "He was found earlier by a worker who came up to check on some of the solar panels. The worker almost tripped over him, scared him half to death, apparently."

"Did he see any sign of anyone else here?" Maya asked.

The sheriff shook his head. "It was all quiet until he found the body."

Maya nodded and stepped into the tent, making her way around the edge of a solar panel. There, she saw the body of a man lying face down on the ground, a length of dark rope still wrapped around his throat.

She'd seen bodies before, plenty of times, but even so, there was a moment of disjunction that always came with seeing the dead. A feeling that something was fundamentally wrong in the world that needed to be put right. A reminder that here was someone who had been walking around breathing and talking until only a little while ago, and whose loss would cause outward ripples of pain affecting everyone around them.

Several of the coroner's people were kneeling by the body, all encased in evidence suits as they worked.

"Is there anything special about the rope?" Maya asked them.

One of them shook his head. "We won't know for sure without analyzing it, but it looks like the kind of thing you could buy at a hardware store."

And there hadn't been anything noted in the files about the ropes used for the other two murders. That made it unlikely that the murder weapon was going to provide a path back to the killer even with this fresh a case.

"We're ready to turn the body," one of the coroner's people said. "On three. One, two, three!"

The techs turned the body, and Maya couldn't stop herself from staring at the man's face. Even with the distortions of sudden, violent death, it was impossible not to recognize it.

The similarity to Howie Barnet, and to Danny West, was uncanny. The same lines of his features, the same shape to the eyes, the same dark hair. This man wasn't identical, but he was similar enough that it was impossible to ignore.

Even Sheriff Lunt seemed to see it.

"Wait, he looks just like the others!"

Maya nodded. "Before, I thought that meant someone was trying to kill Danny West, and then maybe mistook Howie Barnet for him, thinking that he'd somehow survived."

"And now?" the sheriff asked.

Maya shrugged. "I'm not sure *what* to think."

Could it be that some mad person was targeting someone, and kept seeing them in every face that looked a little like them? Could it be that someone had been given a description of a target to kill and was lashing out at anyone in the area who matched it?

No, that didn't make any sense. If it were the latter, then wouldn't the murders have taken place closer together, rather than with such irregular gaps between them?

"Do we have his phone?" Maya asked.

Sheriff Lunt held out an evidence bag containing a phone.

"We'll need to find a way to get into it."

Maya took it and held it in front of the dead man's face just in case, hoping that it would be that easy.

Almost to her shock, it was. The phone's screen came on, letting her into it.

“Facial recognition,” Maya said. It wouldn’t help her for long, though, because she couldn’t stay there with the body of the dead man forever while she checked out the phone.

She took the opportunity to check out the phone quickly. There were messages there from a woman, suggesting how Benjamin had been lured to this location.

Maya took the phone outside with her, out into the sunlight. There didn’t seem to be anything else to gain from staying in there, looking at the body. She could leave that side of things to the coroner and his people. They were far better placed than Maya was to pick through any forensic evidence on the site. Not that Maya imagined that they would find very much. The previous killings hadn’t shown any signs of DNA or fingerprint evidence.

Maya looked around the field, taking in the array of solar panels with the practiced eye of someone who had set up her share of ambushes in the army. While she did so, she kept looking through the phone, taking in the messages, looking at the pictures.

Those were obviously fake. The sheriff had said before that in the Howie Barnet case, there had been stock photographs and an anonymous email address used. Even so, Maya decided to see what was possible to get from the phone.

She used it to call Samit, who picked up after a few rings.

“Hello?” he said in a cautious tone, obviously made suspicious by the unfamiliar number.

“Samit, it’s me,” Maya said. “I’m calling from a phone belonging to a murder victim. Would you be able to access its contents?”

“Hold on,” Samit said. “I’m sending a link through to the number you’re calling on. Click on it. It should give me access to most of the contents of the phone.”

Maya did so. “Look through it, Samit. The victim was lured to the place he was killed by a killer pretending to be a young woman there for a romantic liaison.”

“And you want me to see if it’s possible to trace that back to a real person?” Samit asked.

“Can you?”

“Maybe, but I have to warn you, if this person has been careful, I might not be able to tie the account to anything real. I might be able to link a computer to it once you find the killer, but before that…”

Maya sighed, of course it wasn't going to be that easy. "Just do the best you can."

"I should probably warn you that Agent Harris has been in here, demanding updates about you," Samit said.

"Thanks for telling me," Maya said. She didn't want to say more than that to Samit, certainly didn't want to reveal what she'd found out about the Moonlight Killer, because that would only put him in a difficult position if Harris came around again. "I have to go now."

She hung up. She felt certain now that the connection between the victims was down to their appearance, but she still wasn't sure how that gave her a way into the case. In the meantime, she would keep investigating.

"Sheriff, you said that Benjamin Malt lived on Second Street?"

"An apartment. I have the address."

"And his keys are in evidence?" Maya said.

The sheriff nodded.

Then until Samit got back to her, that was where Maya was going to begin looking.

CHAPTER TWENTY

To Maya, Benjamin Malt's apartment building looked ordinary, nothing special. It wasn't particularly run down, but it also didn't seem upmarket or expensive. It seemed to be in a quiet area of the town, with a few small stores nearby and relatively few people outside on the street.

Maya used Benjamin's keys to let herself into the building and hurried up the stairs to his apartment. She wasn't going there to look for clues to why someone might want to kill him, because the answer to that seemed obvious just looking at him. Instead, Maya wanted to try to work on the question of how the killer was picking out his targets, and if there was anything that might potentially connect back to him.

She was convinced that she was chasing a serial killer now, who picked out his victims for his own reasons. If Maya could establish something about the reasons that the killer was targeting men who all looked so similar, maybe she would be able to get closer to pinning down who he was. She wasn't looking for the reason that Benjamin had been targeted now, just for how the killer had found him.

She reached the door to his apartment and inserted Benjamin's key into the lock. She was just in the process of swinging the door open when she heard the sound of another door opening behind her.

Maya hadn't realized that she was still feeling the aftereffects of her encounter with Gus Scarrat until she found herself turning sharply, her hand already reaching for her gun. She stopped as she saw a woman in her early thirties there, holding a baby. She was a few inches shorter than Maya, with short, dark hair, brown eyes, and a slightly worried expression.

"Who are you?" she said. "You're not Benjamin."

Maya took out her badge. "I'm Agent Gray, with the FBI. Who are you, please?"

"Anita."

"Do you know Benjamin well, Anita?"

"I mean… I guess. We talk sometimes in the hall, and he helped me to move some furniture up the stairs. I've watered his plants when he's been away on work trips."

That caught Maya's interest. "What did Benjamin do for work?"

"Did?"

Maya cursed herself for the slip. "Anita, I'm sorry, I have bad news. Benjamin was found dead earlier."

Maya saw the shock spread across the neighbor's face.

"No, that can't be right. He was… wait, the FBI? Someone murdered him?"

Maya nodded. "Yes. I'm investigating, trying to catch the person responsible. For now, I need to learn more about Benjamin, to try to work out how someone targeted him."

"I… I still can't believe it," Anita said.

Maya wasn't used to this. She worked cold cases. She wasn't used to breaking the news of someone's death to people. She didn't know what to say in moments like this, in spite of her experience as an agent.

"I know it's a shock," Maya said. "Why don't you go back inside? I might need to talk to you shortly, but for now, I need to look around Benjamin's apartment, to see if there are any clues that might point to whoever did this."

She saw the neighbor nod in a slightly stunned way, obviously still not quite taking in what had happened. If Maya had anyone with her, she might have sent them to sit with Anita to make sure that she was ok, but, as it was, Maya was alone. She had to focus on finding the killer, and she was slowly running out of time. It was past noon now, leaving her less than twelve hours in which to find an answer.

Maya headed into Benjamin's apartment. It was clean and neat, with a few pieces of Scandinavian style furniture creating a modern, minimalist feel. There were a few prints on the walls, mostly of cars, while a computer workstation set up towards the back of the apartment had a professional feel to it that suggested either that Benjamin had been a serious gamer or that he spent a lot of his time working there. That caught Maya's interest, because she suspected that she would need access to it if she was going to work out exactly how the killer was finding his victims.

She started the computer up, but there was a password locking it. Maybe she could get Samit to hack into it, but Maya suspected that would take time that she didn't have right then.

Maya hunted through the desk's drawers, hoping that Benjamin Malt would be someone who kept his passwords written down. A lot of people did, reasoning that they could produce more complex passwords and that most of the people who might try to hack into their computer probably wouldn't break into their homes to do it.

Maya got lucky then, finding a small notebook with passwords in it for everything from Malt's email to what appeared to be a dating site.

A dating site? That caught Maya's interest. She knew that the killer had lured both Howie Barnet and Benjamin Malt to their deaths by pretending to be women who were promising to meet up with the men, but was it possible that there was more to it than that. Where might someone look if they wanted to find pictures of lots of men in their twenties, trying to find ones who looked a particular way? Social media, image searches, or a dating site.

Maya needed access to it, but there was a problem, because the one password Benjamin hadn't included was the main one to access the computer. Maya guessed that it was one that he made a point of remembering for security, but that fact made her life more difficult. It meant that unless it was written down somewhere else in the apartment, Maya was going to have to rely on Samit for it and simply hope that he had enough time to do it.

For now, she kept looking around the apartment, trying to get a sense of who Benjamin was. She found a small bookcase with a scattering of books about climbing and hiking that suggested Benjamin liked to be outdoors, but beyond that, there wasn't much that said anything about him.

Maya decided that it was time to call Samit. There wasn't anything here that was going to help her, and…

…wait, what was that, on the far wall? Maya moved closer, trying to get a better look at it. At first glance, she had assumed that it was just another of the prints that sat around the room, but this one was a photograph. It featured a racecar, but also two men standing in front of it. One of them was Benjamin Malt. The other…

…was also Benjamin Malt, or appeared to be. The resemblance was so close that it was like looking at one man twice. A twin brother? In this case, Maya knew that she couldn't afford to take even that for granted. She reached up, taking down the picture, then headed out of the apartment and across the hall. She knocked on the door and Anita answered after a few seconds.

Her eyes were red and Maya guessed that she'd been crying. She guessed that the news of Benjamin's death had come as a shock.

"Agent… Gray?" Anita said, obviously struggling to recall Maya's name.

"That's right. Can I talk to you about Benjamin for a minute or two?"

Maya saw the slight wince on the other woman's face, but Anita nodded anyway, gesturing for Maya to step into her apartment. This apartment was anything but minimalist or neat, filled with children's toys and clothes.

"Sorry, it's all a bit of a mess right now."

"That's fine," Maya said. She followed Anita over to a couch, sitting next to her, the photograph still clutched in her hands. "Can you tell me about Benjamin?"

She wanted to jump in straight away with questions about the possibility of a twin, but she wanted to give Anita at least a chance to talk more generally, and it was possible that any additional information she gave Maya might prove useful.

"He was an engineer, I think," Anita said. "Freelance, mostly. He used to design parts for cars, but anything else that people wanted. He had a small workshop, somewhere."

Maya resolved to have Sheriff Lunt find that just in case there was something relevant there.

"What was he like as a person?"

"He was always so kind to me and little Malcolm. He would come by and see if we needed anything. He was so friendly."

"So he didn't have any enemies?"

"Um… not really. Although he didn't get along with his brother."

"His *twin* brother?" Maya said, holding out the photograph.

"That's right," Anita said. "Zach. The two of them fell out a while ago."

"Do you know what they argued about?" Maya asked.

Anita frowned slightly, as if it didn't quite make sense to her. "It was twin stuff. Benjamin said that he liked hanging out with his brother, dressing the same, doing the same things, but Zach *hated* that. Apparently, he felt like he couldn't be his own person, couldn't be a person at all, when he was around his brother. I heard them argue once. Zach said that it would have been easier if his brother had died racing one of his cars. That way there would only be one of him."

Right there, the faint glimmer of a possible motive showed up in Maya's mind. Was it possible that this was a killer who couldn't deal with other people who looked like him being out there? Was it possible that Zach Malt wanted to be unique to such an extent that now, when he found others who looked like him, he felt compelled to kill them?

To Maya, it sounded like an insane motivation, but to commit a series of murders like this based on nothing more than appearance, wouldn't the killer *have* to be insane? It was also the best potential lead Maya had found so far. She had to follow it up.

She had to find Zach Malt, and urgently.

CHAPTER TWENTY ONE

Megan paced the bunker, going over every inch of it, trying to find something that might help Maya to locate this place. She was tired and her body ached from her captivity, but she still kept going.

Megan was slender and dark-haired, with delicate, almost fragile features that were slowly returning to normal. The bruises that her captor had inflicted on her had faded now, but the memories of his cruelty wouldn't pass so easily.

That was a part of why she walked: it gave her a sense of hope, a sense of control. It said that she was doing something that might help to get her and the others out of there.

There were only four of the others left now: Melissa, Imogen, Lucy, and Adi. Four young women who were all so different, who all came from different backgrounds, yet who all looked basically the same. Their captor had a type, one he'd clearly gone to a lot of trouble to kidnap again and again.

Of course, Megan knew that wasn't the only part of what he'd been looking for when he'd taken them. She'd worked out that each of the women there had been on the verge of changing her life when she'd been kidnapped by the man who held them. Some of them had given up drugs or alcohol, some had been about to go off to school or take up a new career. Megan had come back from traveling and was ready to go to art college.

Megan kept pacing the bunker. She knew the interior of it perfectly now. She knew every inch of it so well that she would probably be able to paint all of it from memory if she needed to. She knew by now that it was very unlikely that she would find any new detail that she could pass to her sister via whichever of the women was released next. She kept looking mostly because Megan needed that element of hope in her life here. She needed the sense that she wasn't completely helpless.

Then she heard the sound of a door opening and all the familiar fears rushed in to almost overwhelm her. As much as she tried to push those fears down, Megan couldn't stop them from coming in every time her captor came here into the bunker.

"Bunnies!" he called out in that too cheerful tone he'd adopted. "Oh bunnies!"

Megan moved towards the large central chamber where a single chair was set up, like a throne. Their captor was already seated on it when she got there, hidden as usual behind a blank mask and shapeless dark clothing. The other women were there, huddled around him, their fear palpable.

"Ah, Megan, dear Megan. Your sister is eagerly going about her business on another case. Just a few more hours to go. Will she succeed this time, do you think? Or will one of these poor bunnies pay for her failure?"

"Maya will solve anything you throw at her," Megan said.

"Are you so sure?" their captor replied, his voice still filled with that fake joviality he used so much to disguise the monster he was.

"I'm certain of it. She hasn't failed so far."

"Ah, the flaw of inductive reasoning. That because a thing has always happened, we feel it *must* always happen. Would you bet your life on it, Megan?"

Megan hesitated, because she knew, with him, something like that was never just an expression. Even so, this was her sister, and she trusted Maya completely.

"I would."

"Good, come with me." He stood then, leading the way through the bunker. He didn't seem to care that Megan was behind him. He obviously wasn't afraid that she might try to jump him and then escape. He had no reason to be. Megan knew from bitter experience that he could fight off her and any of the others with ease, even without needing to use the stun gun he kept on his belt.

He led the way into the room he kept behind a steel door, another circular place, with a bank of screens along one wall showing everything from camera feeds to maps. Megan felt her heartbeat rising as she stepped into that space, because of the smaller circle that sat off to one side, a hook suspended above it, a drain below.

The space he'd set up to murder women.

Only now, it was different. It was worse. There was a wall of chicken wire around it. He'd turned that kill space into a cage.

"I have decided that you will have a new hutch all to yourself, Megan," he said. "You are special, so I should keep you close by. Keep you separate."

Megan swallowed at the thought of that. He was separating her from the others. Had he found out that she'd been passing information to Maya? Was he just doing this to frighten the others?

"Of course, I cannot let you go if dear Maya solves this case. It will be one of the others who goes free. But I have decided to change the rules of the game in one way. From now on, if she fails, it will be you who pays the price. Not any of the others, Megan. You."

Meaning that Megan *had* bet her life. From now on, she realized with terror, if Maya didn't solve a case, Megan would be the one who died.

She just had to hope that her sister was making progress.

CHAPTER TWENTY TWO

Maya had to drive over to the next town to go to see Zach Malt, speeding along the highway as fast as she dared without attracting the attention of the highway patrol, determined to talk to Benjamin Malt's brother as soon as possible.

The decision to do that wasn't easy because it meant committing to a forty minute drive each way. She was eating into more of her brief span of allotted time, getting closer to the moment when the Moonlight Killer would kill one of his hostages with every passing minute.

That brought with it a question: how late should Maya leave it before she abandoned the case and went to try to save the hostages directly? If she realized that she wasn't going to make the deadline, then was there a point where her best chance of saving lives was to try to go to the location she'd found and take down the Moonlight Killer?

Probably, but Maya didn't want to do that too soon. There was still a chance that the Moonlight Killer was playing her with this new information, although it was hard to see how he could have done it. It could be a way to try to get Maya to waste her time on this case, increasing the odds that she would fail to solve it.

For now, at least, Maya was going to continue to work on this case, and not just because it provided a way to get a woman back safely. It also meant taking an active serial killer off the streets, one who had just claimed another victim.

Could it be Benjamin Malt's brother, Zach? It seemed obvious that he hated his brother because of how alike the two were. In a case where the only link between the victims seemed to be their appearances, it was a potential motive that was hard to ignore.

It made the trip impossible to avoid. Maya wanted to sit in front of Zach Malt. She wanted to look him in the eye while she asked him about his brother. If she was right about this, about the reason for the murders, then she wanted to be there to grab him as he tried to run from her. She was taking a risk by using this time, but it was a risk that might get her to the killer.

Those thoughts meant that, by the time Maya pulled up outside Zach Malt's house, she was all but ready to run in there and start demanding answers. She had to force herself to take a moment to look it all over, checking for potential threats and lines of escape.

The house was about as different to Benjamin's apartment as it was possible to get. It was a small, old house on the fringes of the town, with a green square of yard separating it from its neighbors. There was an SUV in the driveway, and Maya thought that she could see movement inside.

He was home; good. The idea of having come all this way only to find the place empty was not one that Maya wanted to think about when she had so little time left.

Maya considered Zach Malt's avenues of escape. The SUV was an obvious one, if he could get past her at the front, but there was also the possibility of him running out through some rear door to the house, trying to escape through the surrounding yards. If Maya spotted that happening, she was confident that she would be able to chase Zach down, but if he slipped out when she wasn't looking, then there was a chance that the head start might prove too much to deal with.

Again, Maya found herself wishing that she had Marco there with her for backup. If he had been there, then it would have been easy to send him around back to cover Zach Malt's potential lines of escape. Instead, she found herself watching the house carefully as she approached, looking for any sign that Zach Malt was about to flee.

Maya had to remind herself as she rang the doorbell that, for the moment, she was just there to question Zach Malt. He was a suspect, but there wasn't enough evidence yet to arrest him. That would come down to how he answered Maya's questions, or failed to answer them.

There was certainly no sign of him coming to open the door. Maya was sure that she could hear movement from inside, but the door didn't open and no footsteps seemed to approach it. Maya rang the doorbell again, calling out this time just to make sure.

"Mr. Malt, this is the FBI! Open the door!"

Still nothing. Seconds ticked by and Maya found her sense of worry about the situation growing. She found herself imagining scenarios in which Zach Malt was already trying to get to a weapon to use against her or in which he was making his escape out the back door of the property.

To guard against that possibility, Maya started to move around the property, heading for the rear of it. She drew her weapon on instinct, half-expecting Zach Malt to come bursting out with a gun in his hands, trying to take her out so that he could get away with murder. Maya advanced carefully, the weapon not pointed ahead of her yet, but she was ready to raise it and fire at a moment's notice if a threat appeared.

She stalked into the rear yard of the house, heading for the back door. There was no sign of anyone running, but Maya still felt a sense of rising tension, sure now that something was about to happen. Maybe it was just how close she'd come to death already today with her visit to *Gus's* bar, but Maya felt the same as she had sometimes in military intelligence, just before a situation turned violent.

Maya moved around to the back door and hammered on it.

"FBI, open up!"

She gave it a few seconds, but there was still no sign of anyone about to open the door. Maya took a step back, ready to kick the door in. She'd lost patience with this, and the fact that Zach Malt was trying to hide from her only made her more suspicious that this was the man who had done all of this. Maya took a breath, started to lift her foot…

…and the door opened, revealing a man who looked exactly like Benjamin Malt. Exactly. Of course, Zach and Benjamin were identical twins, but even details that Zach had control over such as his choice of haircut seemed to be the same. Maya had assumed that he would deliberately dress and style himself as differently as possible to his brother, yet it seemed that the two had settled on essentially the same look.

He also looked frightened, but that probably had a lot to do with the fact that Maya currently had her gun out, covering him. She realized what she was doing and lowered it.

"Zach Malt?" she said. "I'm Agent Gray, with the FBI. I need to talk to you."

"This is about Benjamin?" Zach said.

Maya saw the redness in his eyes then, the look of utter dejection on his face.

"You know what happened to your brother?" she asked.

"Sheriff Lunt of Chelslake called me at work a half-hour ago," Zach said. "I… I can't believe it."

Maya decided to switch to a more conciliatory tone then. She suspected that it would get her more answers than going in and accusing Zach of killing his brother outright.

"May I come in?" she asked. "I need to ask you some questions about your brother."

"I… yes, of course." He stepped back to let Maya pass, then showed her through to a living room where the curtains were half closed. It seemed to Maya that Zach wanted to shut out the world. Zach took a seat in a large, leather armchair, while Maya sat opposite him on a hardbacked side chair.

"I only just got home," Zach said. "When the sheriff called me, I was at work."

"What do you do, Mr. Malt?" Maya asked.

"I'm a biochemist for a local company," Zach replied. "They have a plant just outside of town."

"What time did you get there this morning?" Maya asked.

"A little after eight."

"And you were there until the sheriff called you? You didn't leave?"

"What does… wait, you think I had something to do with all of this?" Zach sounded shocked even by the suggestion of it.

Maya did her best to explain. "I was told that you and your brother had a falling out. That you didn't like being identical to him."

"I just wanted to live my own life!" Zach replied. "That doesn't mean that I would do anything to hurt my own brother!"

"Can you tell me how things were between the two of you?" Maya asked.

"We… didn't speak. I told him years ago that I needed my own space, that I wanted to be my own person. All the time when we were kids, I was always just Benjamin's brother, or one of the twins. Here, I get to be myself. Most people don't even know that I have a brother. *Had* a brother."

Zach put his head in his hands then.

"I wrote to him, you know. Again and again, I wrote these letters, trying to find a way to make things right between us. It wasn't that I didn't want him in my life, I just needed enough space to be my own person as well."

Maya thought that she could understand that, but she still needed to point out what she'd been told.

"I heard that you told your brother that you wished he were dead."

That got a look of horror from Zach. "You don't think I..."

"I don't know what to think, just yet. I'm currently working on the theory that someone is targeting people who look like you and your brother," Maya said. She owed Zach that much of a warning, at least, because he might be in just as much danger as his brother had been. "Mr. Malt, you didn't answer my question before. Were you at work all morning?"

"Yes, yes of course I was. I didn't leave. The lab has security cameras and card readers for the doors. You can check. I was there until the sheriff called me."

Meaning that he couldn't have been the killer.

"Mr. Malt, I'm sorry to have bothered you," Maya said. "I'll leave you for now, but I also need you to be careful."

"Careful?"

"As I said, there's someone out there targeting people who look like you. I don't believe that you're a suspect, but that means that you are a potential target for this man. Try to lay low until I catch him."

"And *will* you catch him?"

"I will," Maya assured him, although right then, she was running out of ideas as to *how*.

She headed back out to her car, trying to think of what to do next. She was almost there when her phone started to ring.

It was Harris. This was *not* going to be good.

CHAPTER TWENTY THREE

Maya got into her car, trying to steel herself before she finally took Agent Harris's call. She knew that it wouldn't be anything good; her boss didn't call her to help with cases these days, only to demand answers and raise suspicions about her methods.

A part of Maya wanted to ignore the call. She didn't have time for this, yet she knew that she couldn't afford to do that. Harris was still her boss, even if she had the autonomy that came from running her own task force within the department. She had to deal with this, and quickly.

"Sir?" Maya said, answering the phone.

"Agent Gray. We know."

Maya could hear something in her boss's voice that stopped her cold, a note of something close to fury.

"Know what, sir?" Maya could feel dread slowly rising within her. After her conversation with Agent Swift, there was only one thing that it could be. Even so, she had to keep up the pretense.

"Don't try to hide it, Gray. Agent Swift has talked to me. She's brought it to my attention that every case you work on looks like the Moonlight Killer, but isn't."

"I know that, sir," Maya said. She had to make it sound as though she was cooperating with her boss, not keeping him out of the loop on the one piece of information that mattered in her case.

"She also asked the crucial question: how does the kidnapper know that?"

"She asked me the same question, sir," Maya said. "I told her that I don't know the answer, and frankly, I don't care. All that matters to me is solving these cases and securing the release of the hostages."

Maya hoped that if she could focus her boss back on the reason why she was on this case, then she could skim past the question of who the kidnapper was for now. She'd been able to use the threat to the hostages and the fact that the kidnapper would only engage with her to get her own task force, after all.

"That won't work this time, Gray," Harris snapped. "Because there's only one answer to that question that makes sense: the kidnapper is the Moonlight Killer."

Maya could hear the anger there in his voice, but also a kind of hunger. He wanted the Moonlight Killer behind bars more than anything, certainly more than he cared about the safety of the women the serial killer currently had as his hostages.

"Sir, that's-"

"Save it, Gray. You know it's true. You *know* it. The only question is how *long* you've known it."

Maya could feel the terror there inside her that all of this was about to be taken away, that she wasn't going to be able to protect her sister anymore. Worse, the Moonlight Killer could very well be listening in to this whole conversation. Just the fact that Harris was saying all of this might be increasing the danger to Megan and the others.

She'd been silent too long now, and she knew it.

"You're done, Gray," Harris said.

"Done? What do you mean 'done?'" Maya shot back. She couldn't let him take her off this case. Not while her sister was still at risk.

"I mean that, whatever excuse you make, whatever arguments you try, this is about the Moonlight Killer. That means that it falls under the purview of Agent Swift's task force. She's going to take over from here on out."

"Sir, I'm the only one the kidnapper will communicate with. The only one who can secure the release of the hostages by solving the cases he sets."

"That is no longer our main priority, Gray," Harris said.

"Saving lives is no longer the FBI's main priority?" Maya demanded. She couldn't keep the anger out of her voice. Agent Harris wasn't just making a mistake now, he was endangering Maya's sister. She would do whatever it took to stop that from happening.

"Stopping the most dangerous serial killer in the country will save far *more* lives," Harris replied. There was no give in his tone, no sense that Maya might be able to persuade him. But then, he'd never wanted the task force anyway. Maya had forced him into it, using the leverage of the threat to the hostages. Now that he no longer cared about that, Maya didn't know what to do.

"Sir, I can do this," Maya said. "I *am* doing this. Marco and I have gotten half a dozen women released."

"And what about the time you solved a case and the kidnapper didn't release anyone?" Harris asked. "What about the times he killed women and just expected you to keep going?"

"He has my *sister*," Maya snapped.

"And that's why you're too close to this to keep working the case," Harris replied. "I should never have let you work it, and now… now, it's over. I want you back in D.C."

"Sir-"

"No! No more arguing, Agent Gray. I am still your superior officer, and I am giving you a direct order. Tomorrow morning, I want you back in D.C., where you will be relieved of your position as head of your task force. You can expect an investigation into just what you knew and when about all of this, too. If I find that you've been keeping me out of the loop, it will be your job, Gray."

Maya could hear that she wasn't going to convince him, and that fact terrified her. She was running out of options, out of chances to make all this right. In that moment, all she could do was fall back on her old training, keeping her tone carefully neutral, making sure that she gave nothing away.

"Understood, sir."

She hung up, and only then slammed her hand into the steering wheel of her car, hard enough that it hurt. Maya felt like crying at that moment, in some combination of anger and helplessness, fear for her sister, and dejection at how out of control everything was. She actually felt the first tears falling down her face, brushing them aside angrily.

"No, I won't let it happen like this," Maya said, but what could she really do? She was off the case. Even if she weren't, she'd just lost her best lead because Benjamin Malt's twin had an alibi. She didn't know what to do next.

No, she couldn't just admit defeat like that. She might be off the case as of tomorrow, but today, she was still in a position to try to catch a murderer. Maya wasn't about to let that go so easily. She still had a few hours. There was still a chance that she could save another woman.

And she had the location of the Moonlight Killer. Maya couldn't forget that. More than that, she wasn't going to simply hand it over to Harris to bungle by blundering in with too many men. She was going to do this *her* way, not his.

First, though, Maya needed help with all of this. She threw her phone into the back seat of the car, hard, hoping that the Moonlight Killer would take it as her simply acting out of anger at Agent Harris.

The moment she'd done that, Maya got out of the car and started to walk, her anger lending fuel to her steps. Taking out her burner phone, Maya called Marco. He answered at once.

"Maya, did you find something?"

"No. Everything… everything's falling apart. Harris just called me. He knows, or he thinks he knows, that the Moonlight Killer is the kidnapper. He… he's putting everything under Agent Swift as of tomorrow. I'll be off the case."

"He can't do that!" Marco said.

"He *is* doing that," Maya replied. "Meaning that I only have until tomorrow morning to make a difference."

"What do you want to do?" Marco asked. No hesitation, he was obviously ready to back her play.

"For now, I need to focus on solving this case," Maya said. "I still have until midnight, but I don't have any leads. I *thought* I had something. This is obviously about the appearances of the victims, because the fact that they all look alike is the biggest connecting factor between them. But how do I use that? I thought I had something with the twin brother of the most recent victim, who didn't want to be seen as just a twin, but he has an alibi, and in any case, I think he's genuinely grieving for his brother." Maya took a breath. "What if all of this is just… random? What if the killer just has a victim type that he likes, and there's nothing more to it than that?"

There was a pause on the other end of the line, presumably as Marco considered the possibility.

"That doesn't work, Maya. How much do these men look like one another?"

"Almost identical," Maya said.

"That's too specific. A killer favoring victims who look a certain general way I get, but if it's one specific set of features, that means something to the killer."

"Such as?" Maya asked. She'd already tried looking for a killer who couldn't stand the idea of other men being out there who looked like him, but without a jealous twin as an explanation, what else was there?

“What if it’s not about hatred?” Marco asked. “What if the killer isn’t trying to kill men who look one particular way because he hates all of them? What if he’s jealous of their appearance?”

Jealousy… Maya considered the possibility, turning it over and over in her mind. Jealousy could be as strong a motivating factor in murder as greed or hatred, could drive people to do unspeakable things. It could definitely work as a potential motive for the killer.

“The only question is how we get from that to the identity of a killer,” Maya said.

“The appearance link must still be the key,” Marco said. “You just need to find a way to pull further on that thread.”

That made sense to Maya, and in that moment, she could think of the perfect way to do it. The only problem was that it would take the FBI’s resources, and using them right now might put her even deeper in trouble.

There wasn’t any choice, though. With her sister’s life on the line, she had to do this.

CHAPTER TWENTY FOUR

Maya felt a sense of trepidation as she called Samit. Would the tech help her now that the task force was being taken away from her? This wasn't Marco, with whom she had a much closer relationship. This was just the tech who had been assigned to her team for the last few cases.

"Agent Gray, what's going on?" Samit asked as he answered the phone.

"What do you mean?" Maya asked.

"I mean that Agent Swift has been in here giving me orders. Apparently, I'm to share everything about our cases with her unit."

Maya sighed; Harris had worked fast when it came to cutting her out. She knew that she owed the tech at least a partial explanation.

"Harris thinks that the kidnapper in these cases is the Moonlight Killer. He's handing the whole investigation over to Agent Swift. As of tomorrow morning, I will no longer be in charge of the task force."

"Just like that?" Samit said, clearly not believing it.

"He's been looking for a way to get control of this investigation again ever since I forced him into setting up the task force," Maya said. "From tomorrow morning, I'm out."

"That's the second time you've pointed out that it's happening tomorrow morning," Samit said, obviously understanding why Maya was saying it. "Does that mean you aren't giving up on the case today?"

"I can't, Samit. There's still a killer out there and there's still a woman's life at risk. I'm going to solve this case before the kidnapper's deadline, regardless of what happens after that."

There was a pause on the other end of the line as Samit thought. "You need something from me."

It wasn't a question.

"I do. Samit, I get that this might put you in an awkward position. Harris and Agent Swift might not like me continuing to investigate here like this."

"You said it yourself: lives are still at risk. Besides, if they ask me, I'll just say that I thought you were still in charge until the morning."

Samit made it sound so simple, but Maya knew that he was taking a risk by doing this for her.

"You might not find yourself fired outright that way, but you still probably won't be Harris's favorite person. It could mess up your whole career."

"This is about catching a killer and saving lives. I'm not about to hold back just because of my career."

"Thank you, Samit. That means a lot."

"Just tell me what you need."

"I need you to run facial recognition on as many sources around the Chelslake area as possible. Search for men who look very similar to the victims in the cases here: Howie Barnet, Danny West, and Benjamin Malt."

"You know the computer will see differences between them, right?" Samit said.

"But you can adjust the parameters to be broad enough to take in all three?" Maya asked. "I'm looking for men who are close enough that they're near matches."

"I… think I can do that. Hold on."

Maya heard the sound of typing on the other end of the call. Samit was obviously running the search.

"Ok, so we need to narrow the parameters down to the local area. We're looking for males who match the photographs. There are a few. Wait, one stands out. I'll send it over."

Maya heard her phone ping as the file hit it. "Thanks, Samit."

"I hope it's enough, because I don't think I'll be able to do anything else for you. There will be enough questions asked just about that search."

"I understand. Thank you."

Maya hung up, checking out the file. It was a mugshot from a DUI that looked far too close to the other victims for comfort, only somehow with an extra edge of symmetry and pristine good looks that went beyond those of the other victims. The similarity was enough that it might have looked like another potential victim, except for one thing.

The file came with a link to a series of online articles about Davis Tockly, a male model who had been in a devastating motorcycle accident just a couple of years ago. Somehow, the press had gotten hold of pictures of him a few days afterwards.

It wasn't pretty. There was scarring all down one side of his face, twisting his formerly good looks into something that almost made Maya gasp to see it. The article speculated on the end of his modeling career, and Maya found it only too easy to believe.

Would *he* be jealous enough now to kill? Jealous of men who had the looks that he'd lost? Unable to bear the sight of them walking around, able to get any woman they wanted online? That seemed to fit with the way two of the victims had been lured to their deaths with the promise of romantic encounters. Had the motorcycle accident pushed him to the point where he would rather kill other men who looked like him than be reminded of what he had before, and what had been taken away from him?

Samit might only have been able to do this one last favor for Maya, but it might have been enough to crack the case wide open.

Maya went back to her car and used her laptop to look for Davis Tockly's address in the DMV's system. He still lived in Chelslake, which meant that she needed to get back there, fast. Throwing the car into gear, Maya set off, determined to get back to the small town before she ran out of time to solve this case.

*

To Maya, David Tockly's house looked like the kind of place that a recluse might choose. It sat at the end of a winding road outside of town, well away from anywhere else and partly surrounded by trees. It looked expensive, the kind of place that a successful modeling career might have paid for, yet it was a long way from being some grand mansion. If he'd ever had one of those, Tockly clearly had to sell it after his motorcycle accident.

Maya pulled up in front of the house, next to an aging muscle car that looked rusty in patches, as if Davis Tockly hadn't been able to afford to keep up the repairs on it. A garage next to the main property was open and almost entirely empty, except for a man working on a motorcycle on a stand. Maya guessed that he had to be Davis Tockly.

The moment he turned toward her, she knew for sure. Surgeons had done a lot to minimize his scars and repair his features, but there was only so much even they could do. The result was that the symmetry of his features was gone, the chiseled jawline now seeming to kink on one side, his dark hair showing a flash of white where a scar cut through it.

Maya got out of the car and approached him slowly, not sure what kind of welcome she would get here.

"You're on private property," Tockly called out to Maya as she approached. "Whatever you're selling, I don't want it."

"I'm not here to sell you anything, Mr. Tockly," Maya said. "I want to ask you some questions."

"A reporter?" Tockly asked. He was half-turned away from Maya now, keeping the un-scarred side of his face towards her. "Another one looking to write a piece about the way my career fell apart? Are you going to tell me that if I give you an interview, you'll help me to get public attention again? Well, I'll tell you now that I don't *want* their attention."

Maya held up her badge. "I'm not a reporter. I'm with the FBI. I need to talk to you in connection with three murders."

That was enough to get Tockly to stop tinkering with his motorcycle and look at her square on.

"Murder? I don't know anything about any murders."

Maya walked forward until she was within the garage, watching Tockly's reactions as she approached. She was looking for any sign that he was about to run or attempt to fight her. If he'd done this and he felt cornered, there was every chance that he might lash out.

"Do the names Howie Barnet, Danny West, and Benjamin Malt mean anything to you?" Maya asked.

"No. Should they?"

"All three of those men have been strangled by an unknown killer. Danny West was killed a year ago, Howie Barnet two months back and Benjamin Malt just yesterday."

"The names still don't mean anything to me," Tockly said. Maya could hear the increasing irritation in his voice. He had a wrench in his hand, which he was using to adjust something on the motorcycle.

"You still work on motorcycles?" Maya said. "You still ride them, even after what happened?"

Tockly snorted bitterly. "It's all I have left. I go to shows, do work on motorcycles. To that crowd, I'm the man so committed to the life that even losing half my face didn't stop me."

He glared at Maya then.

"You still haven't told me what any of this has to do with me, or why you're here."

"You tell me, Mr. Tockly," Maya said. She held up her phone, pulling up photographs of the three victims, one after another. "These are the men who died. Men who look a lot like you used to."

Maya saw the anger rising on Tockly's face. "What is this? You're here to torment me?"

"I'm here to ask you questions," Maya said. "I'm here because you're potentially a suspect in a murder investigation."

"Based on what?"

"On the obvious link that you have to all three victims. Or had." Maya paused, letting that sink in. She wanted to see how angry Davis Tockly could get. "What is it, Mr. Tockly? Did you see them and they reminded you too much of the man you used to be? Couldn't you stand the thought of handsome young men still out in the world who looked almost the way you used to look?"

"You bitch!" Tockly was red-faced with anger then, stepping forward and swinging the wrench.

Maya stepped inside the blow, just barely. She caught Tockly's arm and hooked a foot behind his, sending the pair of them tumbling to the ground. He tried to lash out at Maya with a punch, but Maya stayed on top of him, riding the movement as he tried to buck her off.

As Tockly tried to struggle more, Maya let him turn, going behind him smoothly then driving her hips down to pin him in place. She dragged one of his arms behind his back, then the other, grabbing her cuffs from her belt and locking them onto his wrists one after the other.

"Davis Tockly, you're under arrest."

CHAPTER TWENTY FIVE

Maya stood outside the interrogation room in the sheriff's department that currently held Davis Tockly, trying to contain her sense of frustration at having to wait on the other side of a sheet of one-way glass while he talked to his lawyer. The interrogation room featured gray walls, with a single metal table bolted to the floor and cheap plastic chairs set out around it. Tockly and his lawyer were sitting on one side of that table, deep in discussion.

The lawyer looked a lot less expensive than Maya might have expected from a man who had formerly been both rich and famous, young enough that he was probably just out of law school, wearing a relatively cheap suit and carrying around a battered briefcase. He was currently deep in conversation with his client, making notes as he went.

Maya was so busy concentrating on the two of them there that she barely noticed Sheriff Lunt until he came up to her and put a congratulatory hand on her shoulder.

"I never thought that you would make an arrest in all of this so quickly," he said. "But you did it. You found the one guy with a real motive to kill three men based on nothing more than their appearances."

He sounded so happy about it that Maya guessed that, for him, the rest of the case was a mere formality. It wasn't for her, though. They needed evidence. They needed to be able to show that this was the killer, and they needed that proof before both the Moonlight Killer's deadline and before Agent Harris heard that Maya was continuing with the case.

"We need a confession on this," Maya said. "There wasn't any physical evidence at the scenes to match to him."

"I'll have my guys search his place for the rope as soon as a warrant comes in," the sheriff said.

"But what will that prove? It's a standard rope that you could buy at a hardware store. His lawyer will just argue that plenty of people have it. Without a confession or witness testimony placing him at one of the scenes, we don't have a case," Maya said.

"Then we go in there and we *get* a confession," the sheriff replied, sounding bullish about it.

"We?"

"You don't think I'm letting you go in there alone when it's people in my town who have been murdered?" Sheriff Lunt said.

Maya could have argued that it didn't come down to him *letting* her do anything, since this was an FBI investigation. The problem with that, though, was that the sheriff might try to take up the jurisdiction issue with her bosses. That was the last thing Maya needed, when as far as Harris was concerned, she was done on this case.

"All right," Maya said, "but let me take the lead."

It looked as though the lawyer was ready for them, so Maya headed into the interrogation room with Sheriff Lunt following. They sat on the opposite side of the table from Tockly and his lawyer. Maya noted the way that Tockly angled his face away from the room's security camera, obviously not wanting his scars to be visible on it.

"I demand that you release my client at once," the lawyer said, as soon as they sat down.

"That's not going to happen," Maya said. "At the very least, we have him here for attempting to assault a federal agent."

"We only have your word for that," the lawyer said. "Mr. Tockly is clear that *you* are the one who stormed onto his property and attacked *him*."

"Then there's the three murders," Maya pointed out. "Murders that I was in the middle of questioning Mr. Tockly about when he attacked me. Why did you do that, Davis? Was it because you knew you'd been caught and you were trying to get away, or was it because the sight of other men who look the way you used to just makes you that angry?"

Davis Tockly shook his head. "You were standing there, mocking me, showing me pictures of men who… who hadn't lost everything!"

"Those men are dead, Davis," Maya said. "I'd say they've lost more than you have. And is this you admitting that you lashed out at me?"

"My client admits nothing," the lawyer interjected.

Maya suspected that he should have said something *before* Davis had tried to justify trying to hit her with a wrench. It seemed that Davis really couldn't afford the best lawyers anymore.

"My point is that your client has a trigger that is capable of making him violent," Maya said. "One that means he had a possible motive to kill the three victims in this case. Where were you this morning, Mr. Tockly?"

"Where I always am: at home."

"Can anyone confirm that?" Sheriff Lunt asked, obviously wanting to play his part in the interrogation.

"Of course not!" Davis snapped back. "I live away from people for a reason."

"So you don't have an alibi for the time of Benjamin Malt's murder?" Sheriff Lunt said. "What about two months ago, on the night of the 27th? What about the 15th of August last year?"

"How am I meant to remember where I was?" Davis demanded. "I was probably at home, the same as always."

If he couldn't remember, then he didn't have an alibi for any of the killings. That made him a very promising suspect indeed.

"As far as I can tell," the lawyer said. "You have nothing concrete to tie my client to these killings. Do you have any physical evidence to connect him to all of this? Do you have anything other than sheer conjecture?"

That was the problem: they didn't. Davis's motive seemed strong, he obviously had a temper, and he didn't have an alibi, but that didn't mean anything unless they could connect him to the murders directly. Worse, the lawyer was going to do his best to make sure that Davis didn't accidentally say anything incriminating.

"I'll tell you what we have," Sheriff Lunt said. "We have a witness."

That made Maya frown. "Sheriff, what are you doing?"

"Think about it, Agent Gray. The Danny West case. They said that they thought Danny had gone away and come back, but that's not what happened, is it? That's not what they saw. They saw *you*, approaching, coming to kill Danny West."

Davis was shaking his head then. "No, that's not what happened. That wasn't me."

Maya stood up. "Sheriff, can I talk to you outside for a moment?"

She'd been wrong. She'd gotten all of this wrong, again. She'd brought in the wrong man, and there was no way that Davis could be the killer.

The sheriff looked surprised that Maya was asking that, rather than helping her to pressure Davis into a confession. He still followed her out of the room though, moving away from it with her before he started to speak.

"Why have you stopped?" Sheriff Lunt asked. "We had him right where we wanted him. You agree with me, right? The person who thought they saw Danny West coming back to the restaurant right before his death *must* have seen the killer."

Maya nodded. "I agree with that part. It's a good thought. It seems obvious now that the killer must have looked like his victims. And that's why it *can't* have been Davis Tockly."

"What?" Sheriff Lunt said, sounding suddenly shocked. "You've arrested him, brought him in, and now you're saying that he didn't do it?"

"Think about it," Maya said. "If the man approaching the restaurant was the killer rather than Danny West, then it can't have been Davis Tockly, because he would *never* be mistaken for him, not since his motorcycle accident."

"Unless they just saw him from a different angle," the sheriff insisted.

Maya shook her head. "I don't believe it. It isn't him."

"No, it has to be him," the sheriff said. "He attacked you. I'm going back in there. If you don't want to be a part of this anymore, I can get a confession without you."

"It isn't him, Sheriff," Maya said, but the sheriff was already heading back into the interrogation room.

Maya stood outside the interrogation room, trying to work out what to do next. She felt a sense of dejection at that moment. Like the sheriff, she'd been sure that this was the killer, yet now she was just as sure that he couldn't be. She was still looking for a killer who looked like the victims, but she knew that she couldn't go back to Samit again to ask him to re-run the facial recognition. She had to find a way to do this herself.

Maya found herself running over the facts of the case in her head, thinking about every small aspect of it. There had been three murders, in three separate locations, where the only aspects that seemed to be the same were the manner of the killings and the fact that all the victims looked the same.

No, there was one other thing, wasn't there? Each of the murder scenes had featured something reflective, whether it was the water of the lake, the shining steel of the kitchen surfaces, or the solar panels. The killer had lured the men to specific spots in the case of his last two victims, obviously wanting that reflection to be there while he killed them.

Yet Maya found herself coming back to a different question: how had the killer located his victims? The Danny West murder seemed to complicate it, because he'd been killed at work, without being lured anywhere.

What if that was an exception, though? What if, because it was the first murder, the killer hadn't perfected his methods yet? What did the other two murders have in common? That the two victims had been lured into places with romantic promises.

So what if the killer was finding his victims through the same dating apps that he was using to lure them into position?

Maya needed to confirm which one the killer was using, and after that… well, after that, she had a plan. One that was dangerous, but one that seemed like her best chance right then of getting the answers she needed.

CHAPTER TWENTY SIX

Maya headed back to Benjamin Malt's apartment, letting herself in with the key that had been found on his body. She went back to the drawer where he kept his list of passwords, not caring that she couldn't get in to his computer. She only needed one thing there: the name of the dating site that he'd been using.

She found it written down there with all of the other passwords, and quickly made a note of the address. As soon as she had done so, Maya put in a call to the sheriff's office. Sheriff Lunt answered, which suggested that he wasn't having as much luck as he might have hoped with the interrogation he was trying to conduct.

"What is it, Agent Gray?" he demanded.

"How's the interrogation going? Has Davis given you anything?"

"Are you just calling to gloat about my not getting anywhere?"

"No," Maya said quickly. She needed the sheriff's help. "But you might want to ask him about a dating site called Chelslake Singles. Before you do that, though, do you have Howie Barnet's phone in evidence?"

"Yes, of course," the sheriff said. "We even got it cracked open. It's how we know about the messages that lured him out to the island."

"Can you check it for me?" Maya said. "Check if he used the same app?"

"I… all right, but I don't know what you think you're going to get out of this."

Maya hoped that she was going to get confirmation of the way that the killer was finding his victims. She'd thought it before, when she'd started to think about ways that a killer could find a group of people with a particular appearance. A dating site made absolute sense, because it meant that the killer could filter for different looks, and simply scroll through using a fake account until he found someone whose appearance matched the criteria he was looking for.

The sheriff came back on the line just a few moments later. "Ok, I have the phone here and… yes, it has the same app. But does that mean anything? Danny West wasn't lured out to some special location. He was killed at work."

"I know," Maya said. "But he was the first kill. My guess is that the killer refined his methods after that, realized that he couldn't just walk up to people and kill them wherever they were."

Actually, the Moonlight Killer cases had shown her that a well prepared killer could do exactly that, but it wasn't the approach that this one had chosen. No, he'd identified his victims online, stalked them, trapped them, and killed them in locations that he'd felt able to control, locations where the victims would find their own features reflected back at them in the moments before they died.

"Where does it get us, knowing that the killer uses a particular app?" the sheriff asked.

"For one thing, it should help to disprove Davis Tockly's involvement in all of this. My guess is that he doesn't have that dating app either on his phone or on any computer at his house, and if you ask the lawyer about that, they'll be happy to let you check."

"You really don't think it was him, do you?" the sheriff said.

"It isn't," Maya insisted. "But I think that I might have the means now to get to the real killer."

At least, she hoped that she did.

"All right," the sheriff said. "I'll ask him."

Maya hung up. She wanted to concentrate on what she'd learned, and try to work out how it was going to get her to the killer before midnight tonight. It was still late afternoon, so she had a few hours, but that barely felt like enough now, when she had to turn a connection like this into something that would lead back to the killer.

She knew from the case files that it wouldn't be as simple as tracing back the accounts that the killer had used to a particular computer. That had already been tried, and the accounts had been set up using anonymous emails, so that it would take more time and effort than Maya had available to trace them back to a particular individual, even if she still had Samit's skills to call on.

No, she needed to find another way, and she already had an idea about how that might be possible. She needed to find a way to lure the killer to a particular spot, so that there would be no doubt that it was him.

Yet the only thing she knew about this killer for sure was the kind of victim he favored. The only way to lure him out would be to provide that victim and be there waiting when he tried to make his move.

Maya already had an idea about how she might be able to do that, but it would be dangerous for anyone involved, and it might not even work. The killer had left two months between his last two murders. His need to kill might be sated, for now at least.

No, Maya wasn't prepared to believe that. This seemed like a reactive killer, one who couldn't stand seeing anyone with this particular appearance. She had to believe that if she could create an opportunity for him to make another kill, he would have to take it. He wouldn't be able to help himself.

Briefly, she considered the possibility that she could fake an account, using stock pictures of someone who fit all the criteria that the killer was looking for. It might be the safest option, because it wouldn't put anyone in danger, but Maya was also worried that she wouldn't be able to do it convincingly without full tech backup on this. The killer was obviously familiar with the intricacies of catfishing someone on a dating site. There was a risk that he would be able to spot stock photographs as fake, or that he would wonder how someone new who fit his victim profile had suddenly appeared in Chelslake when they hadn't been there before. That alone might tip him off to the possibility that this was all a trap.

If he realized that, then Maya would never catch him before the deadline. She needed a way to do this that would look natural, and that would have a believable story behind it to explain why the new target was suddenly there in town.

Maya could think of a way of doing it, but it was a risk, one that would place a member of the public in danger. But at least that was a danger that she could manage, try to control. She could keep everyone involved safe and manage to take down a serial killer.

If she didn't, then a woman, possibly even her sister, was going to die. That was a risk that Maya couldn't take, *wouldn't* take. Maya searched for a number and made a call.

The phone rang several times before Zach Malt answered.

"Mr. Malt, this is Agent Gray, the FBI agent who spoke to you earlier."

"The one who pretty much accused me of killing my brother?" Zach Malt did not sound even close to happy about her calling him.

"Mr. Malt, Zach, I get that you're angry, you have every right to be, but the person you should be angriest with is the man who killed your brother."

"Have you found him yet?" Zach Malt demanded.

"Not yet, but I think I have a way to bring him out into the open. The only problem is that I need your help to do it."

"My help?" Zach sounded confused now.

Maya knew that she needed to be honest about what she had planned. She needed Zach to understand what he was getting into. "This killer targets men who look like you and your brother. I've found what I believe to be the site he's using to locate potential victims. I want to give him a new victim, and be there when he tries to strike."

"A new… you mean me? You want to use me as bait?"

It was a word that Maya had been trying to avoid, but the truth was that there was no better word than that for what she had planned.

"Yes, Zach, I want to use you as bait. I'll be there at every step to keep you safe, but I need someone the killer will believe as a real potential victim. I can't just fake it."

"And me coming into town because my brother has died is believable," Zach said, obviously understanding.

"Zach, I could talk to you about the fact that there's a killer still out there," Maya said. "I could say that there are more lives at stake in this, more people who will die if this killer isn't stopped *now*. But I don't think that's what matters here, is it? What matters is one simple question: how much do you want the man who killed your brother brought to justice?"

Maya could guess at the answer to that, because it fit with how she felt every time she thought about the Moonlight Killer, the man who had taken her sister. She would give anything to stop him. Anything.

"I want it more than anything," Zach said. "What do I need to do?"

Maya thought for a moment. "You know your brother's apartment in Chelslake?"

"Yes."

"I'm there. How soon can you meet me here?"

*

The moment Zach Malt walked through the door to his brother's apartment, Maya could see the nerves on his face.

"It's going to be all right," Maya assured him. "There are dangers in this, but I'm going to be with you the whole time. I won't let anything happen to you."

"What do you need from me?" Zach asked.

Maya took her phone and downloaded the dating app. "I need to set up an account in your name, using your email and your picture. I need to use real information so that if the killer looks deeper, he'll find that you're a real person and not someone I made up to trap him."

Zach nodded. "I understand."

Maya took his picture first. That was the hardest part, trying to get a picture that didn't show his nerves or his grief. Then she realized that the killer would be expecting that grief, so it didn't matter if Zach looked slightly haunted in the picture she took for his profile. She would link it to his social media to make it look real, because the killer would spot if this was nothing more than a name and a face. She had no doubt that he would check.

Maya was the one who came up with the profile caption, trying to simultaneously grab the killer's attention and give him a reason to act straightaway.

Just in town for a day. Looking for fun while I'm here.

The killer would know why Zach was in town. He would know that his best chance to kill again would slip away if he didn't act now. Maya set the profile live, and waited, hoping that she was doing the right thing.

She drummed her fingers on the arm of the chair she sat in. How long had it been now? Minutes? More than that? How long could she afford to wait before she got up and tried to get to the Moonlight Killer instead?

"I don't know if this is working," Maya said, but even as she said it, Maya's breath caught in her throat.

Her phone pinged with a message. Someone wanted to chat with the profile she'd just set up.

CHAPTER TWENTY SEVEN

Cillian didn't keep any mirrors in the house, because one look at the sheer wrongness of his features was always enough to send anger bubbling up inside him, impossible to contain.

It had always been that way, as long as he could remember. Cillian's mother had been the first one to point out that he was ugly, that he looked too much like his absent father, that there was just something *wrong* with him.

At first, he hadn't been able to see it, but now that he could, he couldn't un-see it. Even when people told him that he was handsome by every conventional measure, Cillian knew that they were lying. They were just trying to hurt him, trying to make him think that he was mad for not believing them.

He knew that there was something wrong with his appearance, something that could not be tolerated. Why else would his life have turned out the way it had, sitting in darkened rooms, never going out, never able to connect with people except online? Every moment of his life these days was proof of the things his mother had said about the way he looked.

Imagine his surprise, then, when Cillian had found another man who looked enough like him that the two of them could have been brothers. A cook, in Chelslake, at a restaurant Cillian had dared himself to go to in order to try to build up his ability to tolerate the outside world.

This cook had seemed perfectly happy with his life. He seemed as though he had everything. All of that had only fed into the anger Cillian had felt on seeing him. His very existence had seemed to mock Cillian's life. He'd come back a couple of days later, slipped into the kitchen and strangled Danny West while he made him look at the horror that was their shared appearance, using the kitchen surfaces as the kind of mirror Cillian couldn't stand. They had reflected the full horror of Cillian's actions back at him and he'd fled, sure that someone would catch him.

They hadn't, though. He'd gone back to his basement and for almost a year, that had been enough for him. Yet somewhere in the emptiness of Cillian's life, he'd found the need to do something violent coming to him again, the need to spill his hatred for himself out onto someone else before it destroyed him.

The question had been how to find someone else who looked like him, someone else who deserved to die. Cillian had found his answer in the form of Chelslake Singles, the online dating site. It was possible to set up fake accounts and search for whatever appearance he wanted. He'd sifted through the photographs on the site until he found what he was looking for.

After that, it had been easy to lure Howie Barnet to a spot where Cillian could strangle him, the lake providing that oh so vital reflection.

Of course, that had only served to increase Cillian's hatred of himself. He didn't want to be a killer, yet he'd planned a murder and lured a man to his death. Killing Howie Barnet had only made him wish that he were dead, but Cillian had never been able to build up the courage to kill himself. Other men, men who looked like him, had to take his place.

Cillian was still basking in the aftermath of killing Benjamin Malt, but even so, found himself looking over the website, swiping through the rows of pictures, looking for anyone who looked too similar to him. He knew that there wouldn't be since he'd scoured the site just a few days before.

Yet, inexplicably, there was.

Cillian's first instinct was to be wary of this new development. It could easily be a trick, something designed to trap him. The local news had been full of stories on how the FBI had come to town looking for him.

Yet the moment he saw the name on the profile, Cillian found his interest caught. Zach Malt, in town only for a day or two. Could this be… did Benjamin Malt have a twin brother?

Instantly, Cillian went searching online, looking for everything he could find on Zach Malt. He quickly found that this was a real man, not someone the FBI had constructed. This was, indeed, the identical twin of the man he had just killed.

Of course, it could still be a trap, but the moment he saw that Zach Malt was real, the need to kill him overrode that. He couldn't just leave him out there.

Cillian went back to the dating app. He couldn't help himself now. Just the existence of Zach Malt made it impossible for him not to try to correct that. Here was another vehicle for his hatred of himself, ready and waiting to be killed, looking for a hookup even while he was in town dealing with the aftermath of his brother's death and somehow expecting it to work in spite of looking… well, in spite of looking just like Cillian.

He would be careful, of course. He wouldn't give *anyone* the chance to trap him. He was the one who set traps, not others.

Cillian worked quickly, using one of his false accounts, selecting a profile picture and a name that he thought Zach Malt might like, then messaging.

Hi, I'm Beccy. I'm not interested in anything more than one night and I like to be adventurous. Want to meet up tonight?

It was direct, but Cillian had found that direct worked well with these men. Maybe, with looks like his, they were so starved for attention that they couldn't believe it was coming their way, attached to a picture of a good looking young woman. Maybe they were just so arrogant that they believed that they deserved all the attention they got.

Hey, Beccy, that sounds good to me. Want to go out for dinner somewhere?

Dinner? No, dinner didn't work. He needed his targets alone and in a place that he could control. Where, though? He'd already used the field with the solar panels, and there would be cops there still.

His kill on the island, though, had been months ago now. There would be no one there. Could he really kill someone in the same spot twice?

There was only one way to find out.

You don't need to bother with dinner, Zach. We're both grown-ups. We both know what this is, and where it's going.

So, you just want to come over to my hotel? Zach messaged back.

Cillian smiled to himself. He had his target on the hook. Now to start reeling him in.

I was thinking of somewhere else. Somewhere nice and secluded, just the two of us.

CHAPTER TWENTY EIGHT

As she sat in Benjamin Malt's apartment, messaging someone on the dating app, Maya was becoming more and more certain that this was the killer she was talking to. The directness of the approach, the rejection of a hotel room, the hints at wanting to meet somewhere else, all of it seemed to point to the killer's MO, but Maya needed to be certain.

Where did you have in mind? Maya messaged back. Zach was sitting across the room from her, but she couldn't risk letting him be involved in this part, just in case he said the wrong thing and gave away the fact that Maya was laying a trap.

There's an island out on the lake. No one goes there at night now. I thought we could meet there.

The island? He was going to revisit the site of one of his earlier murders? Maya could barely believe the brazenness of it. Yet in some ways it made sense. It was a location the killer clearly knew well, one he felt that he could control and one where the police presence had drifted away thanks to the most recent kill.

All the way to an island on a lake? Maya wrote. *Are you sure it will be worth it?*

Oh, it will. I'll give you an experience that you'll never forget. 10 p.m.?

It was the killer; Maya was sure of it now. She just had to make sure that she did this in a way that meant that she brought him to justice, rather than giving him a chance to escape.

I'm looking forward to it.

"I've set the meeting for tonight," Maya said. She tried to make it sound as if it wouldn't be any problem.

"Are you sure about this?" Zach said. Maya could hear the nerves in his voice. "You're sending me out to meet with… well, with someone who *kills* people who look like me."

Maya could understand his concern. She didn't like this either, sending a civilian out into the field to act as bait for a killer. The only problem was that she couldn't think of another way to catch him, certainly not before the deadline the Moonlight Killer had set.

If she didn't do this, then a woman was going to die.

"I'll be there every step of the way," Maya said. "I'm not sending you out alone. This killer relies on sneaking up on people and strangling them. The moment he tries, *I'll* be the one who sneaks up on *him*. You won't be in any danger."

"I won't be in any danger, waiting for a killer to try to strangle me?" Zach said.

"Not with me there to protect you," Maya said. "This is a killer who needs his victims alone and vulnerable to be able to strike, but you won't be. I'll be watching every moment."

"Just you?" Zach said. "You aren't going to bring in the sheriff's department for backup or something?"

Maya shook her head. That was the last thing she wanted to do in this situation. "We can't afford to bring more people in on this. The killer has picked this place because it's isolated and he thinks he can control it. I'll be able to slip in unnoticed, but if we add another half-dozen deputies to that, all of them making noise as they go, it will be obvious to the killer that we're trying to catch him. He'll just disappear."

"So it's just going to be you and me?"

Maya nodded. "It's the only way to do this."

"I'm… not sure," Zach said.

Maya hadn't considered the possibility that he might want to pull out at this late stage when the meeting was already set. The killer would be expecting Zach to show up, and if he didn't see him, what then?

Could Maya make it work without Zach there? The killer would still be going out to the island, after all. The only problem was that Maya had seen that island; it was filled with potential places for him to hide. She needed to draw him out into the open, and the only way to do that was by having Zach stand there waiting for a woman who didn't exist.

"I know that this isn't easy, Zach," Maya said.

"This is the man who killed my brother," Zach said.

"Yes."

"And you need me there."

Maya wished that she could say no, but if the killer didn't see Zach coming, he would have no reason to show himself. "I do."

Even then, she thought that Zach might say no, but after a few seconds, he nodded.

"All right. For my brother."

Maya felt a moment of relief, quickly replaced by fresh tension. They would be meeting the killer only a couple of hours before her deadline, not enough time to be sure of getting to the Moonlight Killer's cabin before midnight if something went wrong.

Even so, she had to do this. She couldn't just let a killer walk free. They had to get to the island and end this.

*

Maya watched Zach rowing his way out to the island from the edge of the lake, keeping a careful watch for any sign that someone was out there observing him.

Maya had found a small kayak that she could use, sliding it into the water and paddling out towards the island in silence. She hoped that, by coming to the island from a different angle, she wouldn't be easy to spot.

She was dressed, ready for action, with a tactical vest thrown over her shirt. She had elected to leave the standard issue FBI shotgun and long rifle in the trunk of her car, on the basis that Zach's presence in the potential field of fire made them a more dangerous prospect than her sidearm. She'd given him a bulletproof vest to wear under his clothes as a vestige of protection. Maya hoped that it would be enough.

She paddled out to the island with smooth strokes, making landfall on silent feet and dragging the kayak up above the tideline. Maya could see Zach approaching the shore at around the same time, and she edged closer, using the island's trees for cover.

A strange shape loomed out of the dark as Maya advanced, leaving her reaching for her Glock. She only realized as she drew it that it was one of the weirdly constructed statues that artists had been leaving around the island. Maya kept moving forward, trying to keep Zach in sight at all times. She *thought* that the killer would wait until he had Zach in the perfect spot before he struck, but Maya didn't know that for sure and she couldn't afford to take the risk.

Maya could see lights ahead now. They weren't quite by the tower, but instead seemed to be in one of the spots given over to statues and artworks hidden among the trees, a small clearing where strange carved faces stared down from all around. Zach was advancing into that clearing, where it seemed that several mirrors and mirror fragments had been hung, dangling down and reflecting the light of a circle of candles in odd ways.

Maya didn't advance into that clearing. She crouched outside it instead, her eyes roving over the surrounding trees, looking for any sign of movement. Every second or two, her gaze snapped back to Zach Malt, knowing that the killer would head for him eventually.

"Hello?" Zach called out. Maya could hear some of the nerves in his voice. She hoped that the killer would mistake it for excitement. If the killer spotted that he was afraid, then there was a chance that he would realize that this was all a trap.

Maya waited in the darkness, her gun out, watching for any sign of the killer. He was out there somewhere, she could feel it, the tension of staying still building in her, her palms sweating slightly with the nerves that came from having to protect a civilian in the middle of a murderer's trap.

Maya checked the time, ten minutes past ten. That worried her. The killer had said ten p.m., and she couldn't imagine him being late. He wouldn't want to risk his target getting cold feet and trying to leave. So where was he?

Had he worked out what was happening here? That was a possibility that filled Maya with fear. If the killer realized that this was an attempt to arrest him, then he could melt away into the trees on the island and Maya might never catch him. Perhaps he already had. Perhaps, even now, he was making his way back to shore.

The thought of that brought a sinking feeling to the pit of Maya's stomach. If the killer was gone, then her only chance was to try to get to the Moonlight Killer before he could do anything to hurt her sister or one of the others, but Maya didn't have enough *time* to do that. She'd gambled on being able to stop the killer here because she'd been so certain that she could lure him in, but now, Megan might be about to pay the price of Maya's decision.

"No," Maya whispered to herself. "It will work. It has to work."

Maya was still telling herself that when she heard the smallest of sounds behind her. Too late, she realized that, if the killer worked out that this was a trap, then he had another option besides just disappearing into the trees: he could try to kill her first and only then go after Zach.

Even as Maya thought it, she saw something dark flicker through her eye-line, and realized a fraction of a second too late what it was:

The killer was throwing a length of rope around her throat.

CHAPTER TWENTY NINE

Maya reacted on instinct, throwing up a hand as she saw the rope coming down around her throat even though it meant letting go of her gun. The weapon would do her no good if the killer managed to drag her back and choke her into unconsciousness before she could bring it to bear.

She managed to get a couple of fingers in the way of the rope as it went around her neck, but the killer's strength was still tremendous, pulling the rope tight so that it cut into her hand, into her throat.

Maya couldn't breathe at that moment. The killer wrenched her back off her feet even as Maya cursed herself for not seeing the threat coming sooner, for not realizing that a killer who saw her might decide to attack her so that he could get a clear run at Zach Malt. He must have seen her coming towards the island, must have been watching for anyone else approaching, however carefully.

Maya's fingers were in agony as she tried to stop the rope from strangling her. Worse, it wasn't completely working. Maya could feel pressure building up in her head as the oxygen to her brain cut off, and she knew that she only had seconds in which to save herself or both she and Zach might die.

Maya didn't fight back against the pull now. Instead, she went with it, driving back into the killer, slamming her bodyweight into him. She only had one arm free, but Maya used it, driving an elbow back into the body behind her once, then again.

That created some space, just barely enough for Maya to turn in place, facing her attacker and slamming home a couple of punches. She drove a knee into his stomach and *that* was enough to get him to break his hold.

For a second or two, Maya gasped for breath, feeling as though she could barely stand as she threw the rope that had been around her neck aside. Her attacker stood in front of her, and Maya wasn't surprised to see another man who looked almost exactly like the victims. He had the same shaped face, the same build, the same dark hair. He could have been a brother to any of them, except that there was something subtly wrong, something different, in his eyes. Instead, he'd killed them, luring them into secluded spots, and strangling them.

"I won't let you stop me," he said. "He has to die!"

He charged at Maya then, and because Maya was still recovering from the effects of being strangled, it was hard to get out of the way in time. He caught her with a punch that forced her to give ground, staggering back into the candle-lit circle as she tried to recover.

The killer didn't give her any time to do that, though. He just kept coming forward, throwing punches as he went. Maya avoided some and parried others, but inevitably a few got through.

She tried to strike back, lashing out with her hands and feet in an effort to buy herself some time to think. Maya struck the killer in his face with a palm strike, followed it up with a right cross, and then kicked hard at his supporting knee. He barely seemed to notice the blows, as if rage or madness had left him not caring about pain.

Maya looked around for her gun. The Glock lay behind her where it had fallen among the trees, just visible on the edge of the light from the candles. Maya sprinted for it, hoping that if she could get to it she could end this, but the risk was that she had to turn her back on the killer to do it.

Maya dove for her gun, her arm reaching out in a desperate attempt to snatch it up and bring it to bear.

She was just a fraction of a second too slow. She felt strong hands grabbing her leg, dragging her back. Maya kicked out, breaking the grip, but then the killer was on top of her.

Maya had to turn back to face him in order to deal with the threat, getting her legs between her and him but still getting clipped by a punch as her attacker tried to strike down at her. She kicked up, not making contact but at least managing to make him back off briefly.

Maya thought that gave her enough room to stand up, not wanting to stay on the ground with a strong, aggressive attacker throwing strikes at her from above. She put her hand back to steady herself and tried to get back to her feet.

Maya didn't know then whether it was the aftereffects of being strangled or simply that a patch of dirt gave way under her hand, but, either way, she found herself slipping back to the ground unexpectedly.

That gave the killer all the opportunity he needed to slip past the defensive barrier of her legs, throwing a punch as he did that made

Maya taste blood. She clung onto him, trying to find a way to wrestle her way on top, but he was strong enough to hold her in place. He moved to straddle Maya's chest and all she could do was cover up for a second or two as he threw more punches down at her.

Maya felt one of those punches connect with her elbow and heard the killer yelp with pain, yet it still didn't create enough space for her to break free, even if it meant that the barrage of punches stopped for a moment or two.

His hands reached down then, closing around Maya's throat with implacable strength. Maya tried to pull his fingers away but he was squeezing tighter than she could have imagined, with no give in his grip. Again, Maya found herself unable to breathe, and felt the world closing in around her as she faded into unconsciousness.

In that moment, she found herself thinking of Marco, and of Megan. Both of those thoughts gave her the strength to keep fighting, but she still couldn't move her attacker. She could feel her strength fading and…

"Hey! Get off her!"

Zach Malt slammed into the side of the killer in a tackle that knocked him off Maya, leaving her gasping for air as she tried to recover from almost being killed. She saw Zach standing there, clearly not knowing much about fighting, while the killer stood across from him, staring at him with a mixture of disturbed fascination and hatred. It was clear that he hated everything about Zach's appearance, that he couldn't tear his eyes away from the other man.

He lunged at Zach then, his hands reaching out for him to try to lock onto his throat. Zach threw a couple of ineffectual punches, but the killer closed the distance and now the two slammed into one another, going down in a rolling, fighting heap on the ground.

The killer came up on top, and now his hands fastened firmly around Zach's throat. Maya had felt that awful pressure just seconds before and she knew how quickly it could do its terrible work. Zach wouldn't have long before he was rendered unconscious, and it wouldn't be long after that before the civilian died trying to protect Maya.

Maya couldn't allow that. She groaned and rolled to her knees, ignoring the pain and the shakiness that came with it. After nearly blacking out, she felt as unsteady as if she were drunk, but she still forced her way to her feet, not giving in to the almost overwhelming urge to fall back down and lie still until her head stopped swimming.

She took a step and threw herself forward at the killer, latching onto his back and dragging him off Zach with all her weight. Maya stayed behind him, gripping tightly with her arms and legs so that she formed a kind of human backpack, impossible to dislodge even as the killer tried to roll to get her off.

Maya saw the moment when his neck came up in the middle of one of those rolls and her arm snaked under it in a stranglehold. She got her other arm behind his neck for added pressure and squeezed, taking away every inch of space.

The killer went wild in the moments that followed, thrashing about to dislodge Maya, but she held on tightly. His hands reached back for her eyes, but she ducked her head and squeezed her eyes shut so that his fingers merely scraped across her forehead.

Maya felt his struggles weaken, and then finally stop. Only then did Maya dare to let go, still keeping control of the killer as she moved off him, dragging his arms behind his back while he was still unconscious and cuffing them.

"Are you all right?" she asked Zach.

"I… I'm fine. He… he looks just like me."

Maya nodded; he looked almost identical to his victims. Maybe that was the point. Maybe there was something about that lack of uniqueness he couldn't stand, or maybe he hated that appearance. To her, none of that mattered right then. All that mattered was trying to breathe again after almost dying at the killer's hands.

Maya heard the killer gasp as he came back to consciousness, immediately starting to thrash and fight. He glared up, not at Maya, but at Zach.

"You! You have to die! Don't you see how horrific you are? Don't you *know* it?"

Maya held him down, pinning him there while he was cuffed. She got out her phone, calling Sheriff Lunt.

"Sheriff, I have the killer in custody. I'm out on the island and I'll be bringing him in soon, but you should probably get some people down here to secure the scene."

Maya wasn't saying it for the sheriff's benefit, but for the Moonlight Killer's. She knew he would be listening in, and she wanted him to know that she'd beaten his game one more time.

For the *last* time. Maya hung up and then, without hesitation, threw her phone as far as she could in the direction of the lake, hearing the splash as it hit.

CHAPTER THIRTY

There was a postcard waiting for Maya when she returned to D.C., stuck to her apartment door. Maya took it down with some trepidation, expecting there to be a rebuke for throwing her phone away. Instead, there was a picture of a bunny tethered to a post on one side and only the briefest of messages on the other.

Well done. The coordinates are below. From now on, if you fail, it will be Megan who dies.

Maya felt a wave of anger at that, mixed in with the satisfaction that she'd secured another young woman's release. The Moonlight Killer was trying to change the rules of his little game unilaterally, putting more pressure on Maya because now she knew that it would be Megan's life at risk each time. She hadn't thought that it would be possible to hate him more than she already did, but somehow, she managed it.

Maya went into her apartment, changing out of her standard dark suit and into something she could move more freely wearing, settling on dark workout gear with a black hooded sweatshirt. Maya set her gun and badge into place, then went to her wardrobe to grab a couple of extra pieces of equipment.

She drove to visit Marco, parking at the front of the hospital and heading up to the floor where he was staying. A couple of nurses seemed like they were about to tell her that it wasn't an appropriate time to visit, but Maya flashed her badge and they stepped out of the way.

She was a little surprised to see that Reyes was still sitting in the hall outside Marco's room. She'd half expected Harris to pull the protection around Marco before now. Reyes looked up as Maya approached, obviously trying to work out what she was doing there.

"Here to visit the patient?" he said.

Maya nodded. She held up the postcard that had been on her door. "I'm also back from Chelslake. I have the location of the next hostage being released."

"And you're telling me… why, exactly?"

"Because, according to Harris, I'm off the task force first thing tomorrow."

"Sorry to hear that, Gray." Reyes didn't sound as though he meant it. Maya suspected that it wasn't that he disliked her; he just always seemed to think through every situation in terms of the effect that it might have on his career. Maya gave him a second or two to think about the postcard, and how it might look if *he* were the one to rescue one of the kidnapped women, for once.

"Why don't you take the postcard?" Maya said. "I want to visit with Marco, and I guess it's going to be hard for me to take this to Harris right now without walking into a world of trouble. I'd rather save that until morning."

"I'm meant to be standing guard here," Reyes said.

"I don't think there's any more danger now that the Chelslake case is closed," Maya said. "Besides, I'm here. You can call this me relieving you if you like."

She kept holding up the postcard. Maya could see Reyes's eyes fixed on it, trying to calculate just how much credit it would get him to be the one with that information. It only took another second or two before he stood and plucked the postcard from her hand.

"All right, I was getting towards the end of my shift here anyway. I'll say this, Gray, whatever you've done to get kicked off the task force, you at least got those women back."

There was, of course, no hint that her being kicked off her own task force might not be the right thing. Reyes wouldn't go against Harris in anything, at least not until the point when he was in a position to finally take a run at the department head's job. Maya didn't care, though. Asking Reyes not to be over-ambitious was like asking the sea not to be wet. At least this gave Maya time alone with Marco.

He was sitting up in bed when she entered his room. There were a couple of books and some grapes on a table next to him. Maya nodded as she approached.

"Settling in here for the long haul?"

Marco smiled back at her. "They're planning on letting me out of here tomorrow, although the doctors say that I'll have to do rehab and the FBI wants me to see a shrink to make sure that I'm 'processing' all of this properly before they trust me back on duty."

Maya wondered if Harris would use that as a way of moving Marco out of the department without having to go to the trouble of firing him noisily. Just claim that the situation had left Marco unable to do the job and quietly let him go.

"How are *you*?" Marco asked, reaching out a hand to take Maya's. "Did everything go ok in Chelslake?"

"I found the killer," Maya said. "A guy hunting other men who looked just like him."

"The bruises on your neck say it wasn't as easy as that," Marco pointed out. "It looks like someone tried to strangle you."

Maya lifted her hand to the spot where the rope had gone around her neck. "The killer tried. It didn't work."

She left out exactly how close she'd come to dying in that moment, and the fact that she'd been thinking about Marco in what she'd assumed were going to be her last moments. She hadn't been hurt enough to need medical treatment. She'd survived, and that was what mattered.

"Are you sure you're ok?" Marco asked. "If Harris is really going to take the task force away from you and give it to Agent Swift, where does that leave you?"

Maya shook her head. "I'm fine. It doesn't matter."

It was too casual and she knew it the moment she said it. Maya needed Marco to believe that everything was ok, because she knew he would try to stop her if he knew the truth of what she was planning, but she couldn't just come out and say that she was fine. Not when losing the task force would have been a disaster under any other circumstances.

"It doesn't matter?" Marco repeated, giving her a worried look. "Maya, before, you've pretty much told me that being in charge of the task force is the only thing keeping your sister and the other women alive."

"I think I can deal with this," Maya said.

Marco shook his head. "I don't buy it. You must know that Harris won't let this go, and losing the task force is a big deal unless there's something else I don't know about. What's going on, Maya?"

Maya wanted to tell him, but two things stopped her. One was the thought of the Moonlight Killer's postcard depicting this room, the one that had suggested he was watching what went on inside it. It meant that Maya couldn't just come out and say what she was going to do next, because there was a chance that he might hear it and kill his hostages to stop her.

The other was a simple worry that Marco wouldn't want her to do any of this alone. He couldn't back her up himself right now, so he would insist on her telling Harris just to get FBI support. Maya couldn't risk letting Harris know, not when one of his raids would put lives in danger.

"Maya, what's going-"

Maya cut Marco off the only way she could think of, or at least the *best* way she could think of: by kissing him. Her mouth met his, her hand going to the back of his head to pull him closer as she tasted his lips on hers. For several seconds, their mouths explored one another's. Maya finally pulled back, reluctantly, because a part of her wanted to keep going, wanted to stay with Marco all night.

"Everything's fine," Maya assured him. "You get some rest. I'll see you tomorrow."

And if she did everything right, when she did, all of this would be over. Maya left the hospital room, heading back down and out to her car. She started to drive, taking twists and turns to identify anyone tailing her. She couldn't afford to be followed by the Moonlight Killer's people for this part.

Maya didn't like that she'd had to keep Marco out of the loop on this, but no one could know what she was going to do next before she did it. No one could know that she'd found the probable location of the Moonlight Killer's lair before she had a chance to go there and end all of this.

She wasn't going to spend any more time playing his games and hoping that no one died because she was too slow. She wasn't going to dance to his tune anymore. Maya drove off into the night, back out towards West Virginia.

Tonight, she was going to take the Moonlight Killer down, whatever it took.

CHAPTER THIRTY ONE

Maya crept through the dark, approaching the cabin in absolute silence as she clutched a shotgun tightly. She ignored the exhaustion she felt so soon after chasing down another killer. That didn't matter. She was wearing a tactical vest over her workout gear now, her face daubed with camouflage, trying to make her as invisible as possible against the night.

Maya could feel the tension building in her with every step she took. She could see the cabin just ahead, but even now, she found herself wondering if she had the right place.

Then the moon above illuminated the forms of bunny rabbits running across the broad clearing in front of the cabin. Maya felt her anger rising at that too. Bunny rabbits? All this time he'd been taunting her with it, and he was literally giving her a clue as to his location?

That anger almost made her move forward incautiously, but Maya spotted the gleam of a tripwire in the dark just in time. Maya stepped over the trap and kept moving forward, determined not to give the Moonlight Killer any warning that she was coming.

She advanced on the house, approaching it from an oblique angle, watching out for more traps or cameras. Maya spotted one near the door. She knew that when she got there, she was going to have to move quickly, but she took the time to carefully scan the area in front of the door for more traps.

Maya couldn't see any, and she knew that she couldn't stay there forever, because sooner or later the Moonlight Killer *would* spot her with the camera. Maya hurried forward to the door, and since there was no time to pick the lock, she kicked the door hard. Maya heard the lock splinter, the door bursting open.

The space beyond looked like an ordinary cabin, belonging to someone who was into hunting. There were hunting trophies on the walls, the heads staring down at Maya. Weapons hung on racks, while the furniture had a rustic, handmade look to it. Keeping her weapon in front of her, Maya checked the corners, clicking on a flashlight under her shotgun, then moved on quickly.

When she heard the creak of something different under her feet, Maya looked down. There was a rug there, one that looked antique and hand woven. Maya pulled it out of the way on instinct, seeing a heavy trapdoor set beneath.

Excitement filled her, even though Maya tried to keep it in check. This was it! This was the place where the Moonlight Killer was holding her sister. Maya bent to open the door, found another wire, and took tools from her pocket to disarm it. She was working as quickly as she dared now, knowing that there was no time to lose.

Maya knew that this could be a trap, but she still had to move fast. She couldn't waste time now. She plunged down into the space beneath the trapdoor, strip lights coming on automatically as sensors picked up her movement. There was a large metal door at the bottom of a set of steps there, on the far side of what looked like a storeroom filled with supplies to feed… well, to feed a dozen hostages.

The door was locked, but Maya had lockpicks with her. She set to work on it, hearing the mechanism click. She slid the door open and stepped into the space beyond.

Maya crept forward into what proved to be a series of tunnels set beyond. A bunker, but a large one, almost an underground maze. What must it have taken to construct all of this? What kind of effort must it have taken to prepare to take a series of women captive?

Maya kept moving forward, trying to find any sign of those women, keeping her weapon up while she scanned the area around her for potential traps.

She turned a corner and there, ahead, were cages that looked almost like giant rabbit hutches. Most of them were empty but three of them held women, dressed in identical gray jumpsuits. They were all asleep as Maya approached, but the strip lights turning on as Maya advanced roused them. They stared at her in a mixture of surprise, hope, and something like terror, as if they couldn't make up their minds whether Maya's presence there meant that they were saved or doomed.

Maya found herself frantically looking around for her sister. Where was Megan?

"Who are you? You can't… he'll kill us!" She was a young Black woman with a delicate bone structure that reminded Maya of Megan's.

"No one's going to hurt you," Maya promised the three young women. "My name is Maya and I'm with the FBI. I'm looking for my sister, Megan. Is she here?"

"*He* has her," another of the women said. She was in her twenties, white, and blonde haired.

Maya didn't need to be told who *he* was. The kidnapper. The Moonlight Killer.

"And where is he?" Maya asked.

The women pointed along a passageway.

"I'll be back for you," Maya promised. She didn't want to risk letting them out without being able to guide them through the traps outside. She would take down the Moonlight Killer and then lead all of them out of there.

Maya hurried down the corridors, flickering lights starting up above her as she moved forward. There was a broad, open space in front of her, almost circular, with a large chair in the middle of it.

A man sat in that chair, wearing dark clothes and a mask. Was this him? Was this the Moonlight Killer?

Maya started forward, her weapon raised.

"Freeze, don't move!"

Instead of holding still, he moved with the speed of someone long trained in violence. He threw himself behind the chair, firing as he went, gunshots echoing loudly through the interior of the underground bunker. Maya fired back on instinct, throwing herself into cover in the nearest corridor, trying to force her attacker back as her shotgun roared.

"Dear Maya! You've broken my rules!"

Was that the voice of the Moonlight Killer? Was that the voice of the man who had taken her sister from her and forced Maya to jump through every hoop that he put in her way?

Maya didn't care right then. What mattered was taking him down and freeing the women he had as his hostages.

"Where's my sister?" Maya demanded, firing back at him.

More shots came back in reply, forcing Maya to duck out of sight. She had a brief glimpse of the Moonlight Killer retreating into another of the corridors, but she couldn't get a clean shot as he went.

Maya plunged after him into the tunnels, ready to fight, ready to shoot the Moonlight Killer at the first sign of him popping out of cover to attack her.

"Poor Maya, looking for her sister, ready to do anything, ready to risk her life."

The Moonlight Killer's voice echoed around the tunnels. Maya followed the voice, knowing that she had to be careful because this was a very dangerous man, but also knowing that she couldn't afford to waste time. She couldn't lose him.

"You think I don't know you cheated on this case?" the Moonlight Killer said. "I wasn't just watching your phone. I had eyes and ears in the hospital room. You protected your end of the conversation, but not Marco Spinelli's. I don't like cheats, Maya."

There was a flicker of movement in a tunnel to her left. Maya threw herself aside on instinct, but even as she did so, she felt a bloom of pain in her side and heard the sound of a shot.

"Careless, Maya, very careless."

Maya fired back, her shots echoing. She heard the Moonlight Killer giving ground again and followed him, not pausing to check her wound other than putting a hand to her side. It came up bloody. It didn't matter right then. All that mattered was getting to her sister before it was too late.

Maya saw the Moonlight Killer slipping through another metal door. Maya fired furiously, forcing him away from it and kicking the door open.

The room on the far side was another circular one, this one with walls covered in banks of screens. There was a single cage in that room, and in that cage…

"Megan!" Maya called out as she saw her sister. Megan stood there in the cage, but the door was open now and the Moonlight Killer was dragging her out of it with one arm wrapped around her neck.

Maya dropped her shotgun and drew her Glock, knowing that she needed the more precise weapon to have any chance of a clear shot. She circled the cage, trying to find an angle from which she could bring down the man who had tormented her and her sister for so long.

He kept Megan between himself and Maya, though. He wasn't firing back now and Maya wondered if he was out of bullets or if he just didn't want to kill her then.

"Give it up," Maya said. "Let my sister go, put your hands in the air, or I'll shoot."

"You won't risk it," he said. "You should. The FBI playbook says to take the shot if one becomes available, but you won't risk your sister's life. You're a brilliant woman in many ways, Maya, but your need to save others is your weakness."

"There's nowhere for you to go," Maya said. "I can call backup and wait you out."

Maya couldn't see a smile behind the mask, but she could hear the amusement in the Moonlight Killer's voice.

"You really think that I would build something like this that I couldn't get out of?" He brought up a hand. In it was something Maya recognized instantly, something that filled her with fear:

He was holding a detonator.

Briefly, Maya thought that she might have a shot, but could she risk it with her sister there? If she missed, she might hit Megan. She might kill her own sister.

That moment of hesitation was a moment too long. It gave the Moonlight Killer all the time he needed to press the detonator.

Maya heard explosions all around her, the roar of them far too great, the heat of flames springing up and smoke filling the air. Through that smoke, Maya saw the Moonlight Killer drag her sister to a control panel and press a switch.

With a creak, a door opened in the wall, revealing a staircase. Maya saw the Moonlight Killer start to drag her sister up those stairs, heading for the open air beyond as flames started to spring up from the equipment in the bunker.

Her first instinct was to follow, determined not to let her sister go.

Then she thought of the three young women still trapped in their cages in the bunker. Three women who would die if Maya didn't get to them. She hated the thought of leaving Megan in the hands of the monster she was with, but if she followed, then she was condemning three other women to death.

Even then, it took an effort. Even then it took everything she had to turn around.

Cursing, Maya ran back into the bunker.

"We'll see you soon, dear Maya!" the Moonlight Killer called after her as he dragged Megan out of there. "I'll keep Megan *very* safe."

Maya had to force herself to keep running, heading out into the rest of the bunker. Flames were everywhere there, smoke filling the air so that it was getting hard to see. Maya forced her way back to the cages, the three women calling out for help, coughing, and scrabbling at the wire mesh that held them inside.

"Stand back!" Maya ordered them. There was no time to pick the locks on the cages, so Maya shot them, one after another. The locks broke apart as the bullets struck them, letting her kick open the cage doors. She grabbed the women there, pulling them out of the cages one by one.

"Follow me!" she said. "Stay together!"

She started to lead the way back through the bunker, relying on memory to guide her. Maya was coughing now, the smoke growing thick, the heat from the flames almost unbearable. It seemed to take forever to find the stairs that led up toward the outside world. Long enough that Maya found herself wondering if she could locate them at all, or if she and the three hostages would be trapped down there, dying from the smoke or the hungry flames.

When she finally saw the door leading out, Maya pushed the three hostages forward ahead of her.

"Go!" she called out.

The three didn't need any more encouragement, hurrying through the door and then all but running up the steps leading into the cabin. Maya followed them a moment later, the smoke almost too much for her.

Most of one wall of the cabin was gone when she got up there, flames already starting to consume it, obviously trying to destroy any evidence. Maya stumbled out into the open air with the others, sucking in clean air as she led them a safe distance from the cabin.

She looked around for any sign of the Moonlight Killer, but he had already vanished into the night, taking Megan with him. She had saved the rest of the hostages, but Maya's sister was gone, vanished while the cabin went up in flames.

<u>GIRL NINE: GONE</u>
(A Maya Gray Mystery—Book 9)

12 cold cases. 12 kidnapped women. One diabolical serial killer. In this riveting suspense thriller, a brilliant FBI agent faces a deadly challenge: decipher the mystery before each one is murdered.

"Molly Black has written a taut thriller that will keep you on the edge of your seat… I absolutely loved this book and can't wait to read the next book in the series!"
—Reader review for Girl One: Murder

In the Maya Gray series (which begins with Book #1—GIRL ONE: MURDER), FBI Special Agent Maya Gray, 39, has seen it all. She's one of BAU's rising stars and the go-to agent for hard-to-crack serial cases. When she receives a handwritten postcard promising to release 12 kidnapped women if she will solve 12 cold cases, she assumes it's a hoax.

Until the note mentions that, among the captives, is her missing sister.

Maya, shaken, is forced to take it seriously. The cases she's up against are some of the most difficult the FBI has ever seen. But the terms of his game are simple: If Maya solves a case, he will release one of the girls.

And if she fails, he will end a life.

In GIRL NINE: GONE (book #9), Maya realizes that time is running out fast when she discovers new victims of a serial killer left, at each crime scene, with an antique moon dial beside them. This killer must be counting down according to the moon's light.

Yet in a shocking twist, nothing is what it seems.

And Maya realizes, too late, that she herself may just be the target.

A complex psychological crime thriller full of twists and turns and packed with heart-pounding suspense, the MAYA GRAY mystery series will make you fall in love with a brilliant new female protagonist and keep you turning pages late into the night. It is a perfect addition for fans of Robert Dugoni, Rachel Caine, Melinda Leigh or Mary Burton.

Future books in the series will be available soon.

"I binge read this book. It hooked me in and didn't stop till the last few pages… I look forward to reading more!"
—Reader review for Found You

"I loved this book! Fast-paced plot, great characters and interesting insights into investigating cold cases. I can't wait to read the next book!"
—Reader review for Girl One: Murder

"Very good book… You will feel like you are right there looking for the kidnapper! I know I will be reading more in this series!"
—Reader review for Girl One: Murder

"This is a very well written book and holds your interest from page 1… Definitely looking forward to reading the next one in the series, and hopefully others as well!"
—Reader review for Girl One: Murder

"Sooo soo good! There are a few unforeseen twists… I binge read this like I binge watch Netflix. It just sucks you in."
—Reader review for Found You

Molly Black

Bestselling author Molly Black is author of the MAYA GRAY FBI suspense thriller series, comprising nine books (and counting); of the RYLIE WOLF FBI suspense thriller series, comprising six books; of the TAYLOR SAGE FBI suspense thriller series, comprising eight books; of the KATIE WINTER FBI suspense thriller series, comprising eleven books (and counting); of the RUBY HUNTER FBI suspense thriller series, comprising five books (and counting); of the CAITLIN DARE FBI suspense thriller series, comprising five books (and counting); of the REESE LINK mystery series, comprising five books (and counting); and of the CLAIRE KING mystery series, comprising five books (and counting).

An avid reader and lifelong fan of the mystery and thriller genres, Molly loves to hear from you, so please feel free to visit www.mollyblackauthor.com to learn more and stay in touch.

BOOKS BY MOLLY BLACK

MAYA GRAY MYSTERY SERIES
GIRL ONE: MURDER (Book #1)
GIRL TWO: TAKEN (Book #2)
GIRL THREE: TRAPPED (Book #3)
GIRL FOUR: LURED (Book #4)
GIRL FIVE: BOUND (Book #5)
GIRL SIX: FORSAKEN (Book #6)
GIRL SEVEN: CRAVED (Book #7)
GIRL EIGHT: HUNTED (Book #8)
GIRL NINE: GONE (Book #9)

RYLIE WOLF FBI SUSPENSE THRILLER
FOUND YOU (Book #1)
CAUGHT YOU (Book #2)
SEE YOU (Book #3)
WANT YOU (Book #4)
TAKE YOU (Book #5)
DARE YOU (Book #6)

TAYLOR SAGE FBI SUSPENSE THRILLER
DON'T LOOK (Book #1)
DON'T BREATHE (Book #2)
DON'T RUN (Book #3)
DON'T FLINCH (Book #4)
DON'T REMEMBER (Book #5)
DON'T TELL (Book #6)

KATIE WINTER FBI SUSPENSE THRILLER
SAVE ME (Book #1)
REACH ME (Book #2)
HIDE ME (Book #3)
BELIEVE ME (Book #4)

HELP ME (Book #5)
FORGET ME (Book #6)
HOLD ME (Book #7)
PROTECT ME (Book #8)
REMEMBER ME (Book #9)
CATCH ME (Book #10)
WATCH ME (Book #11)

RUBY HUNTER FBI SUSPENSE THRILLER
IF I RUN (Book #1)
IF I TELL (Book #2)
IF I LIVE (Book #3)
IF I FORGET (Book #4)
IF I RETURN (Book #5)

CAITLIN DARE FBI SUSPENSE THRILLER
COME GET ME (Book #1)
COME FIND ME (Book #2)
COME TAKE ME (Book #3)
COME CATCH ME (Book #4)
COME SAVE ME (Book #5)

REESE LINK MYSTERY
BEYOND REASON (Book #1)
BEYOND REACH (Book #2)
BEYOND REPAIR (Book #3)
BEYOND DOUBT (Book #4)
BEYOND NORMAL (Book #5)

CLAIRE KING MYSTERY
ONCE HE SEES (Book #1)
ONCE HE LONGS (Book #2)
ONCE HE TAKES (Book #3)
ONCE HE FEELS (Book #4)
ONCE HE KNOWS (Book #5)

Printed in Great Britain
by Amazon

58121755R00088